The Texas Ranger
and the
Veterinarian

by

Susan Payne

The Texas Ranger and the Veterinarian

Cover Art by *The Wild Rose Press, Inc.*

The Wild Rose Press, Inc.
PO Box 708
Adams Basin, NY 14410-0708
Visit us at www.thewildrosepress.com

Publishing History
First Edition, 2021
Trade Paperback ISBN 978-1-5092-3546-9
Digital ISBN 978-1-5092-3547-6

Published in the United States of America

Dedication

Dedicated to my family for their support and encouragement.

Henry peered up and met Tanner's gaze and all sound disappeared, no more singing or laughter or piano notes. The brightly lit room faded, and there was only the two of them as they were drawn to one another by some unseen force, like a magnet until his lips covered hers and Henry had her first grown-up kiss.

It only lasted a moment, but when Tanner pulled back and stood straighter the light and noise and piano all returned in an unwanted roar, as if they were dropped into some kind of hole with all these other people.

Henry knew Tanner felt the same way. She was sure of it as she touched her lips in awe.

"Don't worry, Henry, your make up is still perfect. I'm sorry. I should have waited to do that," he apologized.

Staring shyly into his shirt, she said, "I really should make myself more available to the reverend. Lure him into trying something."

Tanner's hand tightened a little on her elbow, but then he agreed. "You're right. I admit I can't completely monopolize you or this whole night will be for naught. I'll stay close. Just play with that chain around your neck if you need me, and I'll be at your side before you know."

Making his way to the bar, Tanner watched covertly as she made her way to the table the preacher occupied.

Texas 1883

CHAPTER ONE

Henry wiped the sweat off her brow with her sleeve only to leave a trail of mud instead, but she didn't care. Her physical appearance was the last thing on her mind as she watched the new foal nudge into its mother's underbelly, trying to get the nourishing colostrum to release.

Laughing at the colt's insistence even though it hadn't a clue as to what he was after, Henry shook her head marveling at nature's perfection. She pulled off the long, oiled-canvas gloves that reached her shoulders which she had worn to bring the colt into the world.

A rider had roused Henry from her sleep in the middle of the night as soon as the problem was discovered. The mare, a very expensive dam, had been bred with a very sought-after stud, and the rancher didn't want his prize foal to die during birth. The dam had been having trouble delivering the breech colt, and Henry was the only veterinarian in the district.

Her hair fell free from its no-fuss bun as she washed up in the bucket left for that purpose. She would give a report to the breeder later about the prospects for the colt which were very good now. The dam made it through with flying-colors after a little help from Henry and could be bred again in a year or so. She would recommend closer to two since the dam was so young.

Now the sun was rising, and she was going home to clean-up and get some rest before there was another emergency with the animal population in Connersville.

Removing the blood-stained leather apron, she shook the straw out of her skirts as she left the barn, waving farewell to one of the stable hands working with a yearling in the paddock.

She noticed a stranger on a large roan stallion approaching. He stopped in Henry's path saying, "I'm looking for Doctor Manville. Do you know his direction?"

His badge proclaimed him to be a Ranger, and he had scrutinized her from head to toe as he rode up so Henry did the same to him taking her time before answering him. She noted he was tall, which was the reason for the larger than usual horse, and although the man was trim, his tan trousers, long sleeve shirt, and leather vest couldn't hide his whipcord strength. His ten-gallon hat was worn, but not decrepit, and his boots were at her eye level, expensive and well cared for, the spurs shining in the morning sun.

Finally, she brought her gaze up to meet his, a grin twitching at his lips at her slow perusal.

She answered, "I'm Doctor Manville."

He tried too late to hide his incredulous expression as he made sure she understood who he was searching for. "Wha...Doctor Henry Manville?"

"Henrietta Manville and yes, that is still me." She enjoyed his undisguised expression of disbelief.

He had amazing blue eyes, a few days of blond

stubble on a strong jaw, and firm lips bracketed by lines proving he smiled often. His light brown hair showed under the hat and needed to be cut or it would begin to curl into ringlets. Overall, a very good-looking man and worth Henry's second inspection.

"Sorry, Ma'am," he said touching the brim of his hat a little too late to be polite. "I must have been misinformed. I have a body that needs to be examined before we put it to rest. I apologize for bothering you."

"Wait, who sent you, and where is the body?" she asked before he could rein his horse in a different direction.

Her question stopped his movement. "It's not a nice story, Ma'am. I don't think you want to hear about the death of this woman. She wasn't of, ah, polite society," he explained as courteously as he could.

"You mean she was less than pure? Do you think it isn't worth worrying about catching her possible killer then? That she had no value?" Henry taunted the man, who seemed uncomfortable at being taken to task by a diminutive female.

"I wouldn't have come all this way to find you if I thought the victim wasn't worth my time. And I wouldn't have come all this way to find you if Major Withers had thought to tell me you were a woman," he told her bluntly. "Sorry to have wasted your time."

At the name of the man who gave her a chance before to be of help, she said, "Wait. I'll go with you, but I'll need to pack my equipment. I take it the body was too far away to bring it with you?" She began hurrying toward the horse tied at the hitching post and swung herself into the saddle, settling her skirts down to cover her legs and ankles.

The tall man's mouth was still open. "Ma'am, I don't think you realize I've come over seventy miles. We'll be gone for days. Won't Mr. Manville be worried about you if you just run off?"

"There isn't a Mr. Manville, well, not since my father died so I don't have anyone I need to confer with about what I do in my life. Are you going to follow me to my home, or should you give me the directions and I'll meet you where you need me to be?"

Henry kicked her horse into a trot, and the man followed. Mumbling under his breath words Henry was sure she didn't want to hear let alone know the meanings of.

They were at the rear of her small white clapboard house with a front porch just a few yards back from the road. A stable with hayloft was located behind the house, and a small paddock finished the homestead. A lad of about fifteen came out of the stable and ran up to Henry, a broad smile on his face and a large red dog running next to him with a big welcoming tongue hanging out of his mouth.

"Jason, please watch the place for me for a few days. I should be back by the end of the week. I'll send a wire to let you know if it's otherwise. I'm leaving with Mister ah-h...."

She looked toward the man still sitting in his saddle as he added, "Tanner, Ranger Tanner."

"A real Texas Ranger? We never get anything exciting here. Why are you here then? Somethin' happen I didn't hear about? A bushwhacker gang hiding out nearby? Cattle rustlers? A bank robbery?" The boy kept up a running litany of gruesome occurrences he evidently linked with Rangers.

"Jason, Ranger Tanner came to get me. Now stop bothering the man and let him know where he can feed his horse before coming in for a rest and a meal. I'll be packing," Henry said as she headed into the rear door off a small stoop.

"I'll take your horse, Ranger Tanner, while you go in and rest like the doc says. I'll give him some oats, too," Jason assured as he walked up to the temperamental stallion that let the boy rub his nose and ears.

Tanner watched the horse compliantly follow the boy and smiled. "Sure, kid, he'll be your friend forever." Then followed the doctor into the house.

Tanner found himself inside a neat kitchen with a small table and two chairs, a cabinet with enameled pullout tabletop, wet-sink, and bright yellow curtains. Picking up the coffee pot, he shook it. There was still coffee in it, so he stirred the ashes to get the fire hot and put the pot on the stove to heat. A meal or even coffee would be good before he set out again.

A red longhaired cat sat on the back of the sofa watching his every move then stood, turned with disdain at the interruption, and jumped down to hide somewhere along the short hall.

A much cleaner Doctor Manville showed up saying, a little late, "Make yourself at home. If you're hungry, there's ham in the cooling cupboard and potatoes in the bin. Cook whatever you want, but I'll need to eat, too, since I've been up all night helping at a foal's birth."

Her reappearance knocked a little wind out of his sails making him catch his breath. The pixie-like woman entered the kitchen braiding her strawberry-blonde hair and pinning it on top of her head in a crown without needing a mirror to do so. His first thought was she must do it often or she really didn't care what it looked like—possibly a little of both. He thought it attractive in a kind of just-waking-up in the morning way. Like she was tussled from lovemaking, maybe. Hell, where had these thoughts come from? He had a job to do and then a murderer to catch.

She glanced at him through her lashes. Tanner felt his mouth fall open at the change in her appearance. She was more beautiful now than when he first saw her. Stocking-footed, she wore a split leather skirt, Her long-sleeve shirt was covered by a leather vest with a bright yellow bandana matching the kitchen curtains tied around her long slim neck.

Her sun-bleached hair was already trying to escape from the braid, and her green eyes sparkled as if she was trying to keep laughter under tight control and losing the battle.

He snapped his mouth closed. "I'm a passable cook. All Rangers need to be, or we'd starve. I'll pack up some provisions for the trail while I'm at it, if you don't mind. The Rangers will reimburse you."

"No need for them to do that. If you need me, I'll be packing my gear. I have a few things that will help me make a diagnosis of the cause of death. I take it that is the issue here? No one's sure what caused the lady's demise?"

"Ah, yeah. It's a little suspicious," he told her, still mesmerized by her appearance so close at hand. He was going to need to get himself under control if he was to accompany her to Coyote Gulch and back without embarrassing himself. She didn't seem to be a woman who fooled around, and he wasn't a man to get serious.

The meal was ready to eat about the time Henry came in with a filled saddlebag. "I rolled the glass items in my clothes so they would be less apt to break. I don't suppose we're going anywhere that has an apothecary?"

" 'Fraid not, Ma'am. There's barely a general store," Tanner said as he placed the pan on the kitchen table with a towel under it to save the wood from being charred.

"This looks very good, Ranger Tanner." She pulled out her own chair without hesitation and sat down, picking up her fork at the same time to spear a slice of fried ham.

"Just Tanner will do, Doctor Manville," he said as he sat down across from her.

"And just Henry or Doc will do, Tanner," she said in return as she ate her meal. "I'll give you credit for not burning anything or scorching the coffee."

He ate as quickly as she did, watching her surreptitiously while swallowing his last bite as she finished her coffee.

"That was quite good, Ranger. Thank you."

"It was easy on a stove. Now over an open fire it's a different matter," he told her as he stood and took the empty pan to the sink while she picked up the plates, forks, and mugs.

"I have food for the trip, but only one bedroll," he told her easily, letting her know but not suggesting anything.

"I've got a bedroll on my saddle, and everything else is in these bags." She lifted what appeared to be heavy saddlebags easily after placing a sensible straw sun shade on her head.

The two went out the rear door and met Jason bringing out two saddled horses, Tanner's stallion and a smaller mare that must be the Doc's. Tanner tried not to watch as she pulled herself into the saddle. He took the reins from the boy and mounted easily, the height of the horse perfect for his long legs.

"Get anything you need from the General Store, Jason, and I'll take care of the account when I get back," she called out to the boy as they turned away from the yard toward the road.

"I'll be fine, Doc. Don't worry about a thing." He waved as the riders picked up speed.

CHAPTER TWO

"How long have you been a Ranger? Is this kind of case new to you?" Henry asked as they rode side by side so neither had to eat the other's dust.

"I joined when I was nineteen, a raw recruit just over ten years ago. I wouldn't change things for the world though. It's a life I really love. Freedom to roam, and I like the variety, seeing all parts of Texas, and I still learn new things. I intend on learning from you if you're as good as I've been told. This type of investigation is the first of a kind for me."

"How did you find out about me? Where I was living?"

"My commanding officer, Major Withers, said he's worked with you on a similar case a couple of years ago. Something about the body seemed to make him doubt the death was natural. I'm not sure. I didn't see this body for very long. I was told where you lived and to come and get you if you were available."

"I remember the Major although he was only a Lieutenant at the time. The corpse showed signs of poisoning, and I tracked down the poison and the person who had administered it. I guess I impressed him."

"He didn't hesitate to say you were the one to investigate this death. I know you don't want me to tell you anything about the circumstances, so as not to influence your findings, but from what I was told it doesn't sound like a normal situation at all." After that they traveled in silence, each one lost in their own thoughts.

They stopped a couple of times for water and to rest the horses, but by dusk Tanner said, "We'll have to call it a day. My horse has gone farther than yours, plus I'm a tad bit heavier. Any certain place hit your fancy?"

"Here seems as good as any other. Will we need a campfire?" Henry asked, willing to hunt up something to burn if he needed.

"Not if you don't mind eating ham again. I took yours plus some cheese. I could get fancier if you want. I have some canned goods."

"No, ham and cheese sounds fine by me. Let me walk the kinks out and get Guinevere unsaddled. By then I'll be ready to help with the meal." She dismounted, feeling her legs tremble just slightly before getting her land legs back.

"I'll take care of the horses if you'll go ahead and get the food out of the saddlebag. I'll be ready to eat as soon as I get back. No use in both of us getting our hands dirty when we don't have the extra water to clean up with," he said as he led the horses a few yards away.

Henry searched around for any signs of snakes or scorpions then opened the saddlebag, finding the hunk of ham and cheese wrapped in a towel right on top. Taking out the knife she wore on her ankle knowing it was clean, she carved off a few slices from the ham and quarter wedge of sharp cheddar.

"I didn't make coffee knowing about the water shortage. Did you want me to?" she asked as Tanner came into the small sitting space with the bedrolls and saddles.

He looked at Henry bent over a flat rock where she placed the food.

"No, water will have to do, although it's beginning to taste more like the canteen in this heat," he said setting the saddles opposite each other. No need to cuddle in this heat, either, he thought. A slight dip in the desert temperature could have come in handy about now.

"Not fancy, but there's plenty of it. About how long tomorrow before we get there?" Henry asked as she took a piece of ham piled with a piece of the cheese and bit into it, her pearly teeth sinking into the moist ham then licking her lips as she chewed.

Tanner's mouth went dry—too dry to ever be quenched with water. He cleared his throat, knowing he was letting his imagination be carried away. After all, other than that long perusal of his body at their first meeting, Henry had kept her distance and been all business. She never brought up the fact she was a free woman and he a free man into the conversation or with her attitude. He would have to do the same, but it was going to be more difficult than anything he had ever had to do for the Rangers.

Bringing his mind back to the present, he replied, "By sundown or so if nothing stops us. It took me about two days to get to you. I slept just outside of town last night when I reached it, before coming in this morning and asking for you. Some cowhand sent me out to that ranch."

"I'm going to turn in right now then so we can get an early start. We'll have to let the horses rest along the way. Will we run into any water before then?" Henry asked, seemingly worried about the needs of the horses as she unrolled her blanket and lay down.

Leaning against his saddle, he finished a hunk of ham. "May find some halfway there. Good idea, I won't be staying awake much longer myself." But his words fell on deaf ears as he heard a soft snore coming from the woman who was already asleep after being up most of the night. Tanner felt comforted by the sound and soon lay down on his bedroll, facing Henry.

It took a little longer for Tanner, but he finally fell asleep sometime between wondering what the soap she used was called and wondering if she ever fooled around.

In the morning, Tanner stretched, glancing over at Henry's empty blanket. He saw her coming back from a visit behind a mound of cactus a short distance away and relaxed as she returned to the campsite.

"More ham and cheese? It seems to be the easiest choice," she offered as she shook out her blanket and rolled it up.

"Sure, I'll check on the horses and be right back," he said as he answered nature's call and made sure the horses were ready for another long trek.

It took about the same amount of time to pack up as it did to unpack, and Tanner took his breakfast with him as they rode west, hoping to complete their journey by the time it got too dark to travel. It wasn't going to be a Comanche moon for several more nights so getting to Coyote Gulch would be imperative. The body was on ice but even then, Tanner knew it would be deteriorating and Henry would learn less and less from it as it did.

A few short stops and the two weary travelers arrived at the small town too late to talk with the sheriff and too dark to examine the body anyway. Tanner began to remove the saddles, and Henry looked toward the town. The only thing open seemed to be the saloon. The sound of an un-tuned piano and raucous laughter coming from the area told Henry it wasn't a place she wanted to be right now either.

She peered around the space under the tree Tanner had selected. "I take it there isn't a hotel or anything like that here?"

" 'Fraid not. This is kind of a rough town and mostly used by desperados out of Mexico and other unsavory men looking for a place to hide out for a while."

"But you said there was a sheriff. Doesn't he control things?" Henry asked, not sure what she had gotten herself into.

"He does. By letting them do pretty much what they want to do as long as they don't bother the town's people. The only reason we're here is that the Major happened to be here in town searching for someone when the death occurred. Being a sporting girl, the death would have probably been brushed aside as just one more in a line of deaths among her type." Tanner was collecting dead branches and dried grasses to start a fire then dumped them in a cleared spot. "Instead, the Rangers are involved, and we'll make sure if she was murdered, someone is brought to justice. The sheriff isn't against that. He doesn't want a man here who is a woman killer since it might spread to killing the townspeople. This woman was new to the area, so the sheriff doesn't think of her in the same way."

"Okay, since I'll be seeing the body and hopefully where she died in the morning, you can fill me in on the where and when," she said pulling out a can of beans and the can opener she found next to it.

"I was with the Major, but we got here right after the body was found in a room over the saloon where the girls, ah, where the girls sleep." If Tanner's flushed cheeks were anything to go by, the man didn't feel comfortable explaining anything more about what went on in those rooms.

"I understand, Tanner, I'm not an innocent. These ladies entertain men in these rooms. So, had there been a man with her prior to finding her dead? Who found her and when?" Henry asked as she handed the full can to Tanner with a spoon.

Tanner took a big spoonful and spoke around the food in his mouth while handing the can back to Henry for her to take some.

It seemed an intimate thing to do with a stranger, share food from the same can, from the same spoon. But Henry was hungry and understood the need for convenience taking precedence over etiquette. She accepted the spoon which was still warm from his hand and took a bite of the beans which tasted a little sweeter to her lips.

Tanner continued to fill Henry in on the facts of the case. "She hadn't had a client for a while, and no one can remember seeing her after midnight. The ladies work on the honor method and give the proprietor his share in the morning. When she didn't show up, one of the other girls went to her room and found her dead." He took the can as it was handed back to him and finished it as Henry motioned for him to do.

"How was she found?" At his confused expression, Henry continued, "Was she clothed? On the floor or in bed? Things like that."

"Oh, she was dressed, well as dressed as the girls ever are," he told her bluntly. "But she was laid down on the made-up bed. Now that alone is suspicious since I never saw a sporting girl's bed made in my life." He turned crimson as he imparted this information.

Henry accepted this knowledge with aplomb as she asked, "Is that all?"

"No, she was lying there all serene like. Her hands folded over her waist like you see sometimes in a casket, the body all neat and clean and laying there. It didn't appear anyone murdered her, that's for sure. Kind'a like she was just lying there and waitin' for her end to come." He seemed to be thinking then continued, "It's only because the Major's so adamant it wasn't a suicide we're still working on the case. He said you'd know when you saw her if she died by her own hand or not."

Tanner opened another can, this time peaches which he offered to Henry first. She took a slice and handed the can and spoon back.

Henry deliberated. "I can understand why the Major has his doubt. Someone doesn't simply lie down and die. There has to be more. A poison comes to mind first, but it's very hard to find a poison that doesn't have you retching your guts up before you die. It's not a neat way to go, and lying there writhing in pain doesn't leave a pristine body either."

Tanner flattened the now empty cans, and the two laid down on their separate bedrolls as they had the night before. "This will make more sense to me in the morning. Night, Tanner."

"G'night, Doc. Look forward to learning more about this death tomorrow."

In the morning, Henry came back from her ablutions wearing a clean shirtwaist and crisp bandana. Tanner had changed shirts as well, and they headed over to the sheriff's office. Tanner couldn't help hoping there was a fresh pot of coffee when they got there. Hell, after four days he didn't care if it was fresh, any coffee would be welcome.

Sheriff Ward, a man of medium height and medium looks and medium brown thinning hair, didn't say anything except, "Welcome," when Tanner introduced Henry, but the men's gaze met over their cups of coffee. Message sent and received, Henry was off limits.

"Is there someplace I can set up my equipment? I may need to do an autopsy and investigate stomach contents and such," Henry said in her no-nonsense tone.

"There's a backroom with a separate door on the rear of this building. Usually kept for the deputy, but I'm without one at the moment. Most of them don't like the way their badge seems to be a target when some of the fellas get drunk and bored." The sheriff offered them this information either as a warning or explanation.

"That should do. Can you show me where the body is and the site of the room where the body was found?" Henry began snapping out questions as she began the job she was brought all this way to do.

The sheriff nodded trying to be helpful. "I've got the report from the Rangers if you want to read over that, too. Interviews with the other ladies of the house and a few of the customers to see if they saw anything out of the ordinary. The problem, of course, is that many of the saloon's customers aren't from around here. Many staying for a night then moving on. Very transient so strangers don't draw any notice. I think for the girls, one night rolls into another pretty much the same, so it's difficult for them to say just who was and who wasn't there. We did our best though." Ward took out a file holding quite a few pages and laid it on the desk for her to take if she wanted. She did.

"Thank you, this should help get me started. Is the body nearby?" She picked up the file to read later.

"We kept the body in the ice cave. Doesn't make the town's people very happy, but I told them it was necessary. They would much better like to see her buried and an end to this whole chapter. Townspeople don't like things messy. They would much rather stick their heads in the sand like one of those birds, what are they called?" he asked as he showed her the back room.

"Ostrich," offered Henry reflexively as she glanced over the room and nodded her satisfaction. "Can we walk to this ice cave?"

"Right this way. We can keep ice for months once it's brought in by wagon. The grocer picks it up from the train over in Levenston, and if you keep it wrapped up in straw and burlap it'll last through till fall. Comes in handy in July, I can tell you." He unlocked the thick padded door covering the front of the cave, and all three entered as the sheriff stopped and lit a lantern to guide their way deeper into the rock.

The narrow entrance led into a larger open area where ice was still covered with straw and sawdust to keep it from melting. On the other side of the room was a coffin with the lid on. The sheriff went and lifted the cover so Henry could see the body. As he did so the sheriff told her, "We have a box of personal articles they packed up, too, right next to her. I haven't touched anything, so I don't know what's in there."

The deceased wasn't very big and seemed possibly to be only in her early twenties. Too young to have the rigors of her job written on her face, yet. Tanner was right about that too. She seemed serene, at peace, but Henry doubted the victim put herself in that position.

Henry examined the body noting they had kept her hands folded over her waist just as Tanner had described.

"Could you have the body brought to the back room for me? And the box," she directed the sheriff as he placed the cover back on the small coffin.

As they walked over to the saloon, Tanner seemed to get nervous. "I'm hoping most of the men are still sleeping off their drinks of the night before, Ma'am. As I said, they live rough here."

"Don't worry about me, Ranger. I've been in my fair share of saloons over the years. Can't say they're the safest place on a Saturday night, and I get called in as coroner more often than not."

Stepping onto the boardwalk in front of the saloon, she pushed open the doors bringing in the first slant of daylight to the floor. The smell of stale beer, cheap perfume, and the sawdust strewn across the floor met the visitors. She had smelled worse so wasn't offended by the malodorous interior. The saloon owner was pouring liquid into bottles and replacing the corks as the three entered.

There weren't any customers, at least awake, and

the sheriff explained what they needed. The owner pointed them upstairs.

"You know which room it was. None of the other girls will step foot in there, says they hear Lucy crying or some such stupidity. They won't settle until someone tells them she killed herself and the room isn't haunted or dangerous," he told them but didn't stop working to accompany them.

Henry asked the saloon owner, "Was Lucy quiet or did she seem worried the past few days of her life?"

"No, not that anyone noticed. Some of the girls said Lucy had ordered a new dress and been excited for its arrival. It came yesterday, so I guess she should be buried in it," he said without a lot of emotion.

"May I see it?" Henry asked.

"Sure, I put it up in her room. You can take it with you. Start to help the others forget about her death and all. I haven't had a good night's revenue since it happened," he complained, but stopped when the other three raised their brows. "I mean it will help the girls get back to normal."

When they opened the door to Lucy's room, Henry didn't know what to expect. Red curtains and black laced lamps, but that wasn't the case. The curtains were much the same as one would find in an upscale hotel, a chair covered in flowered chintz. There was a lamp, but it was like what anyone would have in his or her parlor while the rest of the furniture was Spartan.

A bed, of course, and a washstand with bowl and pitcher, and one ladder-backed chair with a table next to it. The bureau with a mirror on top was bare. The box, open on the bed, held a dress that appeared like one a girl in Lucy's line of work would have worn on a regular night. It had a matching feather fan as well as a jeweled piece to pin in her hair.

Henry searched the room but hadn't really thought it would give her much of a feel for the dead woman. Too much time had passed, and others had time to clean-up and remove all the personal items. Knowing how the room appeared would have given Henry a little idea of the girl's state of mind before her death. This room was too clean, or perhaps Lucy herself was always neat and clean. Henry wouldn't really know now. Even people who lived with one another had varying degrees of what was neat and what was chaos.

They left down the front stairs, but Henry noted there was a back set of steps and a rear exit door available. Tanner carried the dress box under one arm, and the sheriff tipped his hat to the saloon owner as they went out through the swinging doors.

"I'll go over to set up my things and wait for Lucy. I hope this will be over in a few hours and we can get her buried properly for all concerned," Henry told the two men as she accepted the dress box from the ranger.

"We'll go and get her and her personal belongings then," Tanner said, about the first thing he had said for quite a while.

It wasn't long before the men were back with the coffin, and Henry made room for it beside the table she was going to use for the autopsy. Henry needed to rule out natural causes like a heart attack or aneurysm. Something that would account for the sudden death of this young woman. As Henry removed the clothes, she noted the body was without bruising or new scars or marks. The woman hadn't met a violent death at least.

Checking for rape was rather redundant so Henry

continued to note the body's color, the stiffness and the color of nails, the texture of her hair, which was bleached. The young woman had probably been hoping for a strawberry-blonde, but ended up with what appeared to be orange, due to the improper use of the peroxide.

Opening Lucy's clenched hand, she found a metal cross, the kind sold at cheap markets, neither of precious metal nor of very good craftsmanship. Henry set it to the side and would inspect it closer later. She continued undressing the body until it was time to begin the autopsy.

Use to the odor by now, Henry said a little prayer as she always did when cutting into a body whether alive or not and began. The heart appeared young and healthy, the arteries showing no sign of damage or poor living. The other organs were as healthy, and Henry was beginning to think Lucy's death was anything but natural.

The uterus showed signs of an abortion or abortions, but that wasn't odd seeing as they would be a side effect of Lucy's career. Once done, Henry checked the contents of the stomach and found what she thought would be there.

Replacing Lucy's internal organs, Henry made neat little stitches to close her up so she would appear natural to anyone viewing the coffin at her funeral. Then Henry redressed the cleaned body in the new dress and began to fix Lucy's hair.

That's when she noticed a fairly large hunk of Lucy's hair had been cut off. It might have been just a lock, but it wasn't in a place a woman would have cut it off herself to give to a lover. The missing lock left a noticeable gap in her hair style. Henry made a mental note to hunt for any signs Lucy had someone in her life who would have received such a gift.

She was going through the last of the items in the box when Tanner arrived to see if the coffin was ready to go back to the ice-cave until the funeral.

"Lucy can go back now. I think I know what killed her, but I want to make sure I'm correct after checking out the dried plants in these jars."

"Do you know what they are? Are they poison?"

"I recognize them, one is Queen Ann's Lace, and neither of them killed Lucy. They are used to bring on abortions for when the ladies of the evening get into trouble. Something no one wants to think about when they're having a good time," she said as she continued going through the clothes and small boxes holding cheap jewelry with fake gems.

Tanner felt his cheeks grow warm. How did this little woman always find a way to make him feel he was in the wrong? That he had lived his life in an insignificant manner? Defensively he pointed out the facts as he saw them. "Most of these women have made choices before they get to a place like this. They decide to enter into this business for the most part, no one held them there against their will."

"If you really believe that, Tanner, you wouldn't be feeling so guilty for visiting women in these sorts of places," Henry said calmly, picking up a locket and opening it to find a picture of a younger, more carefree Lucy.

"I don't feel guilty, not exactly. I never mistreated a, ah, woman like Lucy and I never shorted her payment. I more often left more than she expected.

There's a place, I mean a need, in this world for women like Lucy. It doesn't make them worth more or less than other women, it's just the way life is." He defended himself and the other men who frequented places like the saloon down the street.

"I understand the need, Tanner. There has never been nor will there likely ever be a time when men didn't seek out someone like Lucy. Someone who doesn't expect more than he can give, someone who accepts his needs and wants as passionately as he does, and someone who acts like he is the center of her world, at least while he is with her. I understand the draw and the need to feel like that even if it isn't real," she said as she refolded the clothes and set them into the box on the floor.

"What do you mean it isn't real? It's as real as anything else," Tanner blustered unsure of his footing.

"It's as real as you want to think it, I suppose, but when the next man enters that room after you, his needs and desires are paramount to the woman you just held in your arms. That is, after all, what you're paying her for. Otherwise you would just pleasure yourself and save a lot of money." She stared directly into his blue eyes.

"I don't...I don't need to, to pleasure myself," he sputtered gruffly, unsure if that was what he wanted to convey to her. Now he felt the conversation had gotten away from him after he only came in to find out if she had found the reason for Lucy's death. He felt he had come out looking badly. "I'll get someone to help me take the coffin back to the cave. I'll let them know over at the saloon they can lay her to rest anytime."

"I'm sorry if I've offended you, Tanner. I don't

think women like Lucy or men like you have anything to be ashamed of for living lives different from others. At least you are honest about it. There are some that hide what they are and what they seek. I believe that is what happened here. Lucy was murdered, in her room by someone she had a passing acquaintance with, someone she didn't fear until possibly right at the end."

Tanner left without saying anything more. All he could think was that Doctor Henry Manville was a very complicated lady. He now realized why Major Withers said Henry was the one for this job. Walking to the sheriff's office, he realized there was a lot more to Doctor Henry Manville than one saw at first glance.

Tanner sent a wire to the Major explaining Lucy had been poisoned, but not self-administered. They had no suspects and no reason to think the killer was still in town. They would await further orders before Tanner would escort Doctor Manville home.

As they waited at a table in the saloon later that evening, Henry said, "That was a very nice funeral for Lucy. She made several close friends in the few months she had been here. It was nice some of the customers felt they should attend, too."

Tanner shrugged. "I understand some of the other ladies suggested to their clients that if they wished not to see every one of them go into mourning, everyone that had anything to do with Lucy should show their respects."

"Did you really hear that or are you just trying to be cynical? Don't you think the men who frequent this saloon have any finer feelings?" she asked peering into his eyes to see if he was being serious.

Tanner returned her stare. "Sorry, I'm sure they

would have attended anyway. I just know the other ladies didn't want Lucy's funeral to seem pitiful. After all, it could have been any one of them, and they all know it. And that's without knowing it was murder. I haven't told anyone, so as far as these people know, Lucy simply passed away from some sort of hidden illness."

"That's probably best. I don't think the rest of the ladies are in danger. Lucy was selected for some reason. Perhaps the sheriff will find some clue we overlooked and find out why she was killed while others were left unscathed." She sat up straighter as their meal arrived.

"I never stop in the middle of an autopsy so I missed my midday meal. This steak smells delicious. I only hope the saloon doesn't live up to typical saloon fare." She looked up hopefully. "Well, here it goes."

Cutting into the succulent steak, she put the fork and a small piece of meat into her mouth. Her eyes opened wide, and she smiled in appreciation as she chewed, swallowed, and cut another piece to follow the first.

Tanner chuckled as he cut into his knowing from previous dinners there that the food was pretty good and the steaks superb. "It's good to be in the middle of cattle country when you want a big juicy steak."

"I agree. Why didn't you tell me I had been worrying for nothing? I guess it pays to be the only source of public fare in a town like this. Some of these men wouldn't put up with the food I've faced, sometimes in very nice restaurants. I can taste tainted food immediately, but it's a talent that's saved me from a lot of dysentery over the years," she said as she spiked a piece of fried potato.

Tanner laughed at Henry's ability to look like a lady and talk of dysentery during dinner and not think anything of it. He finished his meal then watched Henry enjoy hers. "Well, you going to sleep in that back room?" he asked her thinking she would take advantage of the privacy and bed mattress.

"No, I'd rather not. The smell of death is still too strong in there, and my clothes probably still reek a little."

"Well I knew it wasn't a new toilet-water, but I was polite enough not to mention it," he said teasing her.

"I guess I'm going to have to wait for a bath. Maybe I can stand out in the open and the wind will help the smell on its way," she teased back honestly.

"I can secure you a bath in the morning at the barber shop. He's not set up for ladies, but I'll stand guard while you use the facilities. Then I can take you home as soon as we hear back from the Major."

"Sounds good to me. I washed-out my other shirtwaist so it will be clean to wear back home. I appreciate the consideration." Wiping her mouth on the napkin, she stood. "I plan on going back to the tree, but you can feel free to stay. I was thinking you may want to give solace to one of the ladies who works here."

The comment caught him off guard since she worded it so nonchalantly. "No, I'm ready to call it a day. After all, we may have a long journey tomorrow if the Major gets back to us early enough." He placed a couple of coins on the table and left.

They spent the night on the hard dirt once again, but Tanner didn't mind all that much because he got to

The Texas Ranger and the Veterinarian

watch Henry sleep across from him. There was no need for a campfire since they didn't have need to keep wild animals at bay this close to town and didn't want to attract the two-footed kind by announcing they were camping there.

He wondered what she thought of his turning down the opportunity of staying with one of the girls at the saloon. Did he rise in her opinion or merely appear as if he were currying favor?

27

CHAPTER THREE

Tanner woke suddenly and pulled his gun at the same time facing it toward the sound that had disturbed him. The sheriff had a sheepish smile on his face and held a pie pan in each hand.

"I knew I should have been whistling or something. Never sneak up on a Ranger when he's asleep. I just thought you and the doctor would like a hot breakfast. I got biscuits and sausage gravy for you." He lifted his hands to show the pans more clearly, but Tanner had already seen them.

By then Henry was awake, sitting up saying, "That was very thoughtful, Sheriff. I appreciate being fed." She smiled looking like a tousled angel, her face surrounded by wisps of strawberry-blonde hair like a halo and her cheeks pink from sleep.

He glanced back to the sheriff in time to catch a look of such longing Tanner found it embarrassing. "Ah, yeah, thanks Sheriff. We'll probably be leaving today, but I need to wait for a wire from my Major first."

"No problem. I'll tell the operators it's a rush when it comes in." Ward handed the pan of food to Henry first then Tanner as an afterthought and stood watching Henry eat in her usual no-nonsense way, savoring every bite and licking the extra off her glistening lips.

Tanner realized he was as bad as the sheriff sitting there watching her chew and swallow, spellbound by the activity he usually wouldn't have given a second thought about. Mentally, he shook his head deciding he wanted Henry alone. "I'll bring the pans back to you after we get cleared-up here. We may as well pack-up and be ready to leave."

The sheriff appeared disappointed, but then smiled and said, mostly to Henry, "It was nice to have your help on the case. I still see no reason to kill a little girl like Lucy, but then who knows what she might have been involved with before coming here. I'll keep all the records for you if you ever want to come back and read through them again."

Smiling, Henry replied, "I enjoyed meeting you, Sheriff Ward, but I hope those papers won't be needed again. I want to think this was someone who followed Lucy from her previous life then slid back into it. I don't specialize in crimes due to mental illness, but her death had a lot of unusual signs of someone killing for a reason other than normal ones. Someone having a sort of contained passion and distorted sort of logic. I would hate to think that person had more victims in their sights."

The sheriff tipped his hat to Henry before adding, "Tanner," in a dismissive manner before striding back toward his office.

"That was a good way to wake up, wasn't it?" Henry enthused placing her now empty pan on the dirt beside her bedroll and climbing out of the blanket fully clothed. "Do you still think you can get me that bath?"

"Sure thing, I'll just go and check that the barber is in, and we'll both get cleaned up." At her shocked expression, he quickly added, "Just not together. I mean I'll get a shave and whatever and you get a bath, alone, while I watch...the door, I mean. While I watch the door to make sure no one gets in." He felt sweat pool beneath his arms as he tried to stop thinking of Henry naked in a bath tub while he watched.

Henry nodded, pawing through her saddlebag searching for her soap and clean shirtwaist saying, "Just as long as the tub's clean and the water's warm."

Tanner got off his bedroll and pulled on his boots then belted on his gun and went toward the saloon and the barbershop next door.

Henry followed him just a couple of minutes later. When she saw him coming out of the door to the shop, she said, "I hope there isn't a problem."

"The entrance for women is through this side door. The ladies from next-door use this facility so it's women only on some mornings, just not this morning. I'll make sure no one interrupts you. Do you need anything?"

"No, I've got everything I need. Do I pay inside?" she asked as she began to open the door.

"No, it's covered by the Rangers. I mean the Major said all costs were to be paid for by me, him, er, the Rangers," he stammered, embarrassed his mind couldn't get past the idea of Henry being naked so close to where he stood. God, he was as bad as a teenage boy watching two dogs hump. Knew it was wrong to stare, but too transfixed on the sight to look away.

Henry's voice interrupted Tanner's reverie. "I'll have to thank him then. This is a real treat, and I swear I can still smell death all over me." She entered the room and closed the door on a now quiet Tanner.

There was no lock on the door, and she realized that was why Tanner was standing guard. The door to the barbershop did have a lock, which Henry went over to and turned.

The walls' rough wooden boards showed mildew growing in the corners and up the sides from the wooden floor. It was Spartan, but for the two tin tubs in the center. Only one contained water so Henry removed her clothes hanging them on one of the hooks for that purpose. She noticed a large pitcher of warm water next to the tub she would use to rinse her hair and stepped into the tub with her bar of soap.

Henry felt like a new person after her bath. The odor of death was gone as well as that gritty feel to her hair from the dusty trip to Coyote Gulch. Even knowing she was going to have the same dusty trip back home didn't lessen the fresh feeling she had right then. After braiding her hair, she bundled her soiled clothes and soap and unlocked the door to the barber's shop. Going out the side door, she almost walked on Tanner as he sat on the step into the building.

"All done. The room's all yours if you want it," she chirped happily.

Standing up quickly, he asked teasingly, "Thanks. Is that just a polite way to say I'm getting ripe? Smelling more like my horse than my horse?"

"Well, nothing makes you feel better than being clean, and I saw that you brought a clean shirt with you. Do you want to use my soap?"

"No, I got some already, but you do smell real nice." He leaned toward her to catch a whiff. Then was sorry because his mind went right to lying beside her, his nose in her hair, his hands on her breasts, his hips pressed into hers. But then something interrupted his dream.

"I said," began Henry evidently for the second time, "then I'll go finish breaking-up camp and taking the pans back to the sheriff." He saw she was watching him closely.

"Right, I'll just take that bath." He turned quickly, rammed into the door, then opened it before he made more of a fool of himself.

Once inside, Tanner leaned back against the closed door and willed his body to calm down and certain parts to relax. The barber was coming in with hot water and pouring it into the still damp tub, and Tanner made a silent groan. He would not think about the fact a naked Henry had just sat where his naked butt was going to be, that the warm moist air hadn't caressed her body earlier, that the wet footprints leading to the hooks weren't hers. God, this was going to be a long bath to get through.

Tanner took one of the fastest baths ever, including the one he took in the middle of December in a half-frozen river. His dirty shirt rolled up in his large hand, he hurried back to the camp to help Henry and to take back the pie pans to the sheriff. Instead, he found Henry returning from the sheriff's office, a slip of paper in her hand.

She waved it in the air. "A wire for you. I didn't read it, but I know what it says because the boy bringing it evidently reads all the wires before delivering them."

"That's good to know. I'll make sure to let the main office know to tell them to seal all correspondence from now on." Tanner unfolded the paper to read his orders. "So, are you available to ride to Willowbrook with me? A death with similarities to this one is only a few miles away. Makes one wonder, doesn't it?" he asked, his brows raised in question.

"Almost forty miles, but yes, I'll wire Jason to let him know I won't be back as soon as I thought. It will make his day since he likes to stay at my house with the animals. He's one of nine children, and his family has a small farm outside of town. It's rather crowded as I hear tell. This way, he can help out there when he's needed, but have a room and bed of his own plus all the loving from that big dog you met."

"I'll get some supplies from the general store here so if we don't end up going through towns we can at least eat well," Tanner said, shaking out his bedroll and making it ready to tie onto his horse again.

It took the two of them a little over two days to get to Willowbrook, and Henry stated she was more than ready to be reintroduced to modern conveniences like a tub, pumped water, and food not eaten out of a can. Tanner volunteered to take both horses to the livery while Henry registered at the hotel nearby. He wasn't sure if he was going to camp out, sleep at the livery, or stay in a room like a regular person.

Tanner decided to stay with the horses and let Henry stay in the hotel. The building was clean, and the restaurant wasn't too bad or too expensive, and it furnished great coffee. Henry cleaned up in the hotel bathing facilities while Tanner visited the barber again and felt almost human.

Over breakfast together they discussed what to do since this death hadn't been ruled a murder, just a suicide. The Major had been searching for any similar deaths to Lucy's and found this one had occurred only a week after hers.

"Do you think the sheriff will be open to our looking into this death? I mean, aren't we kind of telling him he did a bad job?" Henry questioned as she devoured one of the biggest breakfasts Tanner had ever seen.

"Well, that's why we have to move gently. Some sheriffs don't like Rangers messin' in their jurisdictions at all while others wait for us with open arms. I've never had a call to come here before, and the Major wasn't very open on how he found out about this woman's death."

"Then let me take the lead," she told him. "I'll ask as a coroner to define what killed her. If the body hasn't been buried, I can get what I want to know simply by looking at it."

"All right, we can always fall back on demanding if that doesn't work," he said finishing his coffee.

When they found the young sheriff in his office, Tanner let Henry do the introductions, leaving out the fact they just came from investigating a similar death and had ruled it a homicide.

Tanner was amazed at how Henry used her womanly wiles without seeming to, but he knew this wasn't her normal posture, her normal way of speaking. He wondered if she had ever done something similar to him then decided he would have recognized false praise and a fluttering of eyelashes if she had. Anyway, he hoped he would have.

Sheriff Brand, blushing with pride that Henry was interested in his work and this case, was falling over his own feet to help her examine the body still in the mortuary waiting for the girl's family to come and pick up. Her name was Mary Foster, and she had been working in the brothel for over four years so didn't seem to have any crossover time with Lucy.

In fact, Henry told Tanner to go to the brothel and find out what he could about this poor young woman's life there and before she came to Willowbrook.

Entering the dark basement of the building, the smell of decaying human flesh was prevalent and familiar. Henry asked if she could be alone with the body, explaining she wouldn't disturb the young woman in any way. Merely wanted to study the effects of poison on a human and any other pertinent information. The inexperienced sheriff was a little green already and quickly left Henry with the body without further discussion.

The woman now in front of Henry could have been Lucy's older sister, the build was similarly petite and not too bosomy. There were no signs of bruising or restraints. As Lucy was, this girl's hands were positioned across the waist and folded together and that is how the mortician left her. Her hands were empty, but there was a cross lying between her breasts. The same design and quality she had found in Lucy's hand.

Finding the gap where a lock of natural strawberry-blonde hair had been cropped led her to a conclusion. Henry didn't need to do an autopsy to know this was a homicide and it had been committed by the same killer who murdered Lucy.

She asked a couple of questions of the mortician about the condition of the woman's body when it was brought in and if the cross was in the woman's hand originally. The answers matched what Henry knew of Lucy, and she thanked the overly thin man for his time.

Sitting in the front lobby of the hotel, Henry waited for Tanner to show so she could confirm their beliefs about the dead woman. The town was quite busy with wagons and buggies going to and from the business section. Across the street, a boy was pasting up posters for a powerful elixir that would cure anything and everything over those of the tent revival from last week's entertainment.

Henry hated those snake oil salesmen who preyed on the sick and often addicted. She knew alcohol made up most of the ingredients, while often poison or other evils made up the rest. The only reason people didn't die more often was that they passed out before consuming the entire bottle.

Tanner came down the boardwalk, his long legs eating up the space between them, and Henry felt a little shiver go through her body at the sight of him. She didn't have time to question her body's response to him, but she did enjoy seeing his smile as he entered the hotel foyer. He spotted her sitting at the window seat and turned toward her.

"That took you long enough. I suppose you had to taste the wares to keep your cover?" she teased, half wondering if that wasn't what he had done as he blushed.

"No, those ladies work late so they don't get up very early. I spent the time talking with the bouncer." Henry's brows drew down in thought, so Tanner explained, "Usually a big guy who protects the girls from anyone roughing them up or leaving without paying. He was full of stories, but most of them you wouldn't be interested in." He smiled as he seemed to remember some of them.

"By the look on your face, I would say you might be wrong. I might be very interested in some of his stories." She watched his eyes as he hid under the brim of his hat.

"I'll save those for a lonely night out on the trail, but it boiled down to no strange occurrences before or after her death. Just some Bible thumpers trying to get the ladies to change occupations and find religion. Bunch of hypocrites. The bouncer tells me he saw the preacher there every night that tent was outside of town, and he wasn't trying to change the girls' mind about anything except the amount he was willing to pay."

"Really? And you don't find that strange?"

"Revivalists? No, they're all over this time of year while it's still warm and they can get to towns having their centennials and such. Fourth of July is always big, lots of ranchers coming in to town, of course. There was one in Coyote Gulch just as we arrived."

"You mean just before Lucy was murdered?" Henry watched his face change as he registered the timing.

"Too much of a coincidence don't you think? I'll wire the Major and ask if there were any similar deaths in the past and if there had been a tent revival or something related occurring about the same time." He got up to send the wire directly from the station rather than from the hotel's front desk.

Henry followed him out then strode across the street to peel the new poster off so she could read the one underneath. The one advertising the tent revival and found what she needed. The revival had the name of the preacher, a Reverend Ambrose Agape, which she knew meant love in the Bible.

So, what did Mrs. Agape think about her husband's wanderings at night after the show? Was she aware he was using, then killing, these women? Probably not. Wives have been known to not notice when things aren't right between themselves and their husbands.

The cross should have been a giveaway, except the Major hadn't said one was found with the other homicides across the state with which he had become familiar. Of course, they had been closed as a suicide, and now all these types of cases would need to be re-opened and investigated. Since these women were all hookers, there was no one to demand justice. Henry didn't care what these women chose to do in their life, she felt their early death should be avenged just as any other.

Returning to the hotel, she became antsy waiting for Tanner. Instead of waiting, she walked the few blocks to the brothel to speak with some of the ladies who she felt must be awake by now. Henry was correct, although she had to argue and persuade the large man guarding the door she wasn't a disgruntled wife hunting for her missing spouse. Nor was she a jealous wife about to pull the hair out of one of his women's heads.

Once inside, Henry was pleasantly surprised at the cleanliness of the foyer and parlor although she could smell the lingering aroma of whiskey and cheroots. There were two round tables with chips and cards stacked neatly in the center surrounded by several chairs as well as more conventional parlor furniture covered with brocade and rich velvet. Seeing a red velvet curtain hiding the hall and stairs to the upper rooms, she wondered how far she could get before the bouncer tossed her out.

The gilt mirrors on every wall would reflect the light from the crystal chandeliers as well as show off the ladies from all sides. Men evidently met and mingled here before making a selection for the night, or the hour, if Henry's information was correct. There were several framed oil paintings of inadequately dressed women on the walls also, some appearing as if they had just rolled out of bed. A few tables holding decorative lamps and standing ash trays were beside each sofa lining the walls.

A tall, elegant woman appeared from behind the curtain wearing a stylish day dress with large bustle and scooped neckline, both appropriate for being seen on the town's boardwalks. She was older than Henry, but her smile was real, and her blonde hair appeared real while her brown eyes were watchful.

"I'm Lillian, and I'm the madam around here. I understand you have questions about Mary? That you work with Tanner and are considering the possibility Mary didn't take her own life?" she asked bluntly.

"I am working with Tanner, and neither of us thinks Mary took her own life. Do you?" Henry asked just as bluntly.

The older woman answered slowly, measuring her words. "I think there are women who are cut out to be in this business and those who aren't. I don't hire the ones who aren't. I was completely taken aback by Mary's death, but there weren't any signs of her being murdered. I assumed I must have missed something, missed the signs she was unhappy or distraught."

The woman took a deep breath showing the worry

was real. "We are a very empathetic group. We share everything with each other and help one another through any low points. It's not always an easy life." Lillian watched Henry closely, probably for any signs she found the conversation distasteful or crude.

"I understand, and I'm glad to hear you shared with one another. Does that mean if Mary or any of the ladies here felt uncomfortable with a man, she would tell you or the man at the door?"

"Normally me first, and I would involve Bruce if need be. Usually it was a man too drunk to finish and blaming the girl or wanting more when his allotted time was up. I could usually persuade most men to sleep it off, and he'd be right as rain in the morning. No one wants to get banned from the place. We're the only whorehouse in this area." Lillian laughed a little at her use of the word, and Henry knew it was probably only to see if the woman could get a rise out of Henry.

"Not a fate a man would want to incur, I'm sure." Henry tried to ask the right questions now she had the woman's trust. "Did Mary say anything about a man making her feel uncomfortable, too preachy, or trying to convert her from her 'wicked ways'?"

"I know what you might be getting at. There were a couple of women who came one day and tried to get all the women to attend a revival meeting in a tent just outside of town, but none of the girls took them up on the invitation. It's not as if my ladies don't know about God—merely that they don't think God condemns them to hell for what they're doing. I mean there's that whole part about Sodom and Gomorrah, and we feel we're simply doing our part in keeping men from lying with other men." The madam smiled then asked in a friendly manner, "Would you like some tea?"

"Normally, I would say yes, but I made a pig of myself at breakfast and am paying for it now." Henry felt she needed to explain. "We had been on the trail for so long that all the food on the bill of fare sounded good to me."

"Well, I wouldn't have worried about food either if I were alone on the trail with Tanner. He's one fine looking man. How do you keep your hands off him?"

"I don't think of Tanner in that way. He's my bodyguard, I suppose, you could call him and, although he is great to look at, he's a little too chauvinistic for me. Little woman belongs in the kitchen, that sort of thing. Anyway, I live many miles away and he lives wherever the Rangers send him," she explained, thinking she was honest with her answer and her feelings.

"Too bad." Then Lillian stopped and asked, "Bruce told Tanner about the preacher who kept coming here, didn't he?"

"I was most interested in him, yes. Did he ever, ah, select Mary? Were there other girls who caught his attention?" Henry asked trying to see if her hunch was correct.

"Well, let's see. He was here several nights in a row. First there was Mabel then Ester, but then he seemed to settle on Mary for the last three nights," Lillian said, peering up into the air trying to remember for sure.

"What do the other two look like? Any similarities to Mary?"

"They all have red hair depending on the henna, only Mary's was natural. Small build yet curvy, some men call them a pocket Venus, and they all sang and were educated to about the sixth grade. They all had been in the business since their late teens, been knocked around a little until they came here. That's about it," the madam said, and picking up her hands dropped them into her lap emphasizing that was all there was.

"That's enough. You've been a great help, Lillian. I can assure you Mary did not take her own life. She was targeted because of how she looked as well as the fact she was available. I hope to have the man rounded up in the near future, but without more evidence, we'll need to almost catch him in the act."

Standing, Henry picked up her gloves from the sofa's seat. "At least we know where he will be going next, and the murders always seem to occur near the time, when he is leaving town. Possibly trying to hide his sin so to speak. I don't know why, and we may never know, but we are a lot closer to catching him. The Rangers always get their man," Henry quoted to Lillian. "Thank you for seeing me. It has answered many of my questions."

There was a commotion at the front door and Tanner, followed by Bruce, came storming in, his gaze surveying the room, stopping when it came to Henry. Upon seeing she was all right, he expelled the breath he was holding.

"I thought you were going to stay at the hotel. It took me a while to figure out you had come here. I wasn't done telling you what I had found out and you hare over here the first chance," he reprimanded her. She knew it was for frightening him and not for leaving the hotel.

"I was speaking with Miss Lillian, Tanner, and I

think we are on the right trail now. We'll fill in the Major, but we need to follow that tent revival and in particular the Reverend Agape. I think he may be the killer," Henry pronounced.

"Let's make sure before we let it out, we've got the guy," Tanner said finally able to take his gaze off Henry and turned toward Lillian for confirmation to his request. "If Miss Lillian and Bruce would keep this information close to their chests, I'd appreciate it."

"Of course, just let me know when you've got the son of a bitch and we'll hold a celebration to his hanging." Smiling she turned to Henry and said sotto voiced, "You'd be a fool to waste this chance. Good things are few and far between in this world, and many never get a second chance at happiness."

Henry nodded in agreement and followed Tanner outside where the bright sunshine hurt her eyes after the darkened parlor. "I didn't mean to take so long, but I got the information I needed. Did you hear back from the Major?" she asked to keep Tanner from yelling at her anymore.

"He sent a message by return wire almost immediately. Had the information we asked about and had it all lined up. There are three others, all the same, all thought to have been suicides so there weren't any open cases. We need to get to this minister and stop him. I'd arrest him now except we haven't very much besides hunches and the fact he was seen with the victims, but never right before they were found dead." Tanner explained his problem, which Henry had already figured out.

"Let's go to the next town advertised on their tour and see what we can do. Possibly follow him around the clock, and before he can take a girl to a private area, we stop him and find the poison on him." Henry was spouting out ideas as fast as she could think of them. "Confront him with the facts we have and see if he will admit to the murders, tell him he needs to ask for forgiveness for his sins or burn in hell. Tell him anything to get him to confess."

Henry kept up with Tanner's long strides that he finally shortened now they were away from the brothel.

"Having him know we're on to him may make him lay low for a while, but he seems a little crazy to me. Only a hangman's rope is going to stop him I'm afraid," Tanner said.

"How long will it take us to get to Melville? That's the next stop. We can attend a meeting and check out this reverend and maybe any other men who travel with the show. You know, roustabouts, men who put up the tents and drive the wagons. There might be others who will need watching."

"You needn't worry about the men. You were brought in just to check the bodies, and that's all I'm letting you do. The Major will have my hide if anything happens while you're under the Rangers' care."

CHAPTER FOUR

Tanner and Henry set out knowing they wouldn't get to another town before dark set in. At least, this time they could stick to the roads and have the chance of stopping for water at a local farm or ranch. Tanner bought more supplies and Henry added to her wardrobe, just a couple of shirtwaists and socks that would fit into the saddlebag without being completely crushed. Tanner added another shirt and called it good.

The first night they set up camp they ate a cold meal out of the cans, sharing as they were used to doing and minimizing the need for plates and flatware. It was too hot for a campfire, and there were no wild animals to ward off. Tanner lay on his side, facing Henry as he liked to do while Henry, a few feet distant, curled away from him.

The morning began as usual followed by long hours in the saddle. The hours were passed with conversations about favorite books and stories of their favorite teachers and family members. They felt comfortable with one another and Henry, who was more talkative than him and always seemed interested in people, shared some of her history and asked questions about his.

Henry had several professors who had odd little ways, and Tanner told her of his younger brother and sister and how much he missed them due to his job as a Ranger. Both his parents were still at home running the ranch while his siblings grew up without him. But his parents were close with him, and he enjoyed his time off when he visited them.

Stopping off to get water at local ranches, the horses were able to go further in a day. Even though it was hot after the long cooling drinks, the water didn't need to be rationed as it had to be when going cross country. The couple didn't spend too much time at these farms because the sooner they had eyes on the revival tent the sooner they would catch the killer. Then Henry and Tanner could return to their normal lives.

One night while still on the road to Melville, Tanner touched upon a subject that had been bothering him. "Henry, you talk about your professors and some of your anatomy classes and such. Aren't those classes for doctors? I mean people doctors? Is that why you're sometimes called in as a coroner?"

Henry hesitated, seemingly having difficulty finding the right words to explain her whole life. "I studied to be a physician, like my father, but gave it up after a couple of years. Then people began to ask me to help them with their pets and animals, and I felt more comfortable doing that. At least, I haven't wasted my education completely."

"But isn't it a waste when you use only part of that education to help others? I mean I know a lot of men who are great with animals without ever going to school. Just know when a horse is getting down or if a calf is sickening. You have more education than that, but you don't seem to want to use it. I know you're not squeamish so what's the reason?"

He watched her expression as the sun set behind her, making it more difficult to read her emotions, but was sure there was something she was hiding.

"It's complicated," she stated pulling out her blanket and removing her boots.

"Then un-complicate it for me."

Again, Henry was silent and as Tanner almost repeated his request, Henry started quietly. "I was a new doctor, only twenty years old, and I was out to save the world. I took over a small medical office from a retiring doctor, and before I knew it, I had more patients than I could count. First time mothers and dying grandfathers. I handled it all without a qualm. Feeling omnipotent that I could handle anything.

"Then they brought me, Martin. A ten-year-old boy, Martin had been happy and rowdy like his four siblings until one day his mother noticed that his bruises weren't healing like his brothers did. He was getting tired sooner, sitting out of the usual rough-housing the other children were into. She brought him to me because she thought he needed a tonic, something to boost his energy and make him stronger."

Tanner remembered her adamant hatred of the snake-oil salesmen and type of magic elixir sold to the unwary. He felt staying silent and letting her tell the story was going to be cathartic for her in some way although he feared where this story was going to end.

Henry continued quietly, "His mother had tried some through the newspaper advertisements, but they seemed to make him worse, so she finally talked her husband into letting her bring him to me." She stopped speaking, and he could see she was remembering another time, another place while staring into the night sky.

"And you couldn't help him?" guessed Tanner.

Now there were tears in her eyes, the glistening showing in the moonlight as it began to shine in the sky's darkness.

"It seemed like what I suggested worked for a while. He got a little stronger, went back to school, and was more interested in learning about the farm again. Then he began a downward slide, passing the point where I first started seeing him and losing ground daily. The mother was beside herself with worry, his father was sure it was something I had done or not done. After all I was just a young woman to him.

"He wanted the retired doctor to come back and see to his son. I was in correspondence with the old doctor and he called it the wasting disease and there was nothing that could be done. He had seen it before, but not for many years. It simply seemed to pick out someone and they ended up dying. There was no cure, no other end for it."

Tanner was sure Henry was crying now, and he felt like a cad for bringing her to tears just so he could get to know her better, to get closer to her.

"I'm sorry, Henry. I know you tried your best. If you couldn't fix him there wasn't any way anyone else could either." And he believed his words. No one gave more to a job than this woman. No one cared about others more than her.

"I know that. I do." He could tell by her manner that this wasn't the first time she had tried to convince herself she wasn't at fault and not the first time she had failed to do so. "It was a form of cancer called leukamie. One we have no way of cutting out of

48

someone. A kind with no cure, no way to make better or change the outcome. But knowing that didn't make the pain in those parents' eyes any easier to live with, to not feel some guilt at my inability to save him." Sniffling, she wiped her eyes on her sleeve. "I was a doctor. I accepted payment from people who had done nothing, besides gotten ill. How dare I call myself a healer if I couldn't guarantee I would heal them? I felt like a fake, a fraud."

Now Tanner could hear the sobs caught in her throat as she went on, almost in a whisper, "If a foal dies at birth, well the rancher's out the cost of a stud fee. If a child dies, it robs the whole family of part of its life. I can't be responsible for that again."

Tanner lay back on his bedroll wishing he smoked, wishing he had asked her any other question than the one he had, although now he felt closer to her than ever. Maybe in her confidence she became closer to him. He hoped something good would come out of making her feel so badly.

"Goodnight, Henry, and I'm sorry about Martin," was all he could think to say. Henry remained quiet.

Neither of them mentioned the confession of the night before although Tanner tried to be more solicitous, breaking up camp when Henry went to relieve herself and saddling the horses without any assistance, usually something they did together.

That day was spent pretty much like the others. The two horses walking side by side down the road which was still dry and dusty with little hot puffs of wind blowing across the couple, making them put up their bandanas to keep the sand out of their mouths. It was uncomfortable riding and made communication difficult, so Tanner didn't learn any more about this woman he found fascinating. He didn't want to stop, though, because the revival tent was set to move on after only two days in Melville, and they were more than two days behind the minister's group.

That evening during supper, not able to stop thinking about his traveling companion, Tanner began his questioning again. "That town I found you in, how long have you been there?"

Henry swallowed the mouthful of canned meat and thought a moment before saying, "I bought the farm about three years ago. I wasn't sure what I was going to do, but I couldn't stay where there were so many bad memories. Then Jason came and volunteered to help take care of my horse, and he had a sickly goat he brought with him to care for during the day. I examined the pet and called him Merlin because he had one horn out of his forehead, and he was like a mystical unicorn. Merlin was the only mystical name I could think of."

"So, you cured him?" asked Tanner unnecessarily because, of course, she saved the dumb animal.

"Yes, then he brought me one of the rabbits they keep. It was only an infection of an eye. Probably scratched by one of the other rabbits. He was getting older, and the younger males were trying to drive him out of the warren."

Tanner couldn't stop himself. "So, what did you name him?"

"You're beginning to learn my secret. I name most of my patients depending on their temperaments. I called him Sir Galahad since he seemed like a gentleman and was good to the ladies." He noticed she blushed as she realized what she had said.

"And a veterinarian was born?" Tanner teased.

"Not until I was brought a dog that'd been bitten by rattlesnakes saving the children of a family after they inadvertently walked into a snake den. That dog jumped between the snakes and the children and grabbed any snake that had the audacity to leap toward them. He killed several before the children's screams brought their father and he began shooting the rattlers until they all slithered away under the rocks. The children were unhurt, but the dog…." Tanner could see her shake her head slowly. "I wasn't sure I was going to be able to save him."

"But you did," stated Tanner, certain of the answer.

"Yes, but the family needed to move on. They were settlers going west into California, and the dog wasn't going to be well enough for days. At that time, we weren't even sure he was going to live, but he was a hero, and you never give up on heroes. The children left him in my care and told me I could adopt him when he got better. Jason became quite attached so, of course, I kept it, too. Just the start of my menagerie." She smiled speaking of her misfit animal farm.

"So, Jason had a full-time job taking care of all these adoptees?"

"It became that way little by little. At least I haven't adopted him. His mother's rule is he can stay the nights at my farm when I'm not there, but otherwise he's to be home with his family," she explained to Tanner. "After saving the dog, the rest of the town seemed to accept me as their animal doctor, and I didn't mind that title at all. I like all my patients, and they are always grateful for my care because I usually make them feel better than when I found them." She finished her meal, leaving the spoon jangling against the side of the empty can.

Tanner nodded accepting her story and seeing how her life had become what it was when he found her. He noted with satisfaction she never mentioned a man or any real ties to the farm other than the animals that he could move to wherever he finally ended up.

And that's when Tanner realized he was trying to find out more about Henry because he was thinking of what was to happen after this case was solved, after the killer was arrested and the Rangers sent him on another assignment. He liked the idea of having Henry waiting for him after a long difficult case.

Laying back against his saddle, he watched as Henry settled herself for the night, accepting every discomfort and lack of amenities as well as any Ranger ever did. The moon showed her eyes closed, their lashes fanned out on her cheeks, the wisps of hair curling to frame her delicate face.

Tanner stopped there. He didn't want to keep listing her attributes or he wouldn't get to sleep this night at all. In fact, too much talk of her may have already put paid to a long night's rest. He found his mind wanted to return to her story of her animals and her farm and even her eccentric professors.

He realized he liked to think about her. Liked the way his body took notice of her even as she slept across from him. What would it feel like to have her nestled close to his body? Her stretching as she woke up, pushing her breasts into his back, or better yet, his chest as they slept face to face.

Now he had gone and done it. Body parts he didn't

have a way to relieve were making themselves known, just because he thought about this delectable little morsel of a trip companion. Tanner gave a deep moan rolling to his other side hoping by not being able to see her, his body would relax and he could sleep. He knew now it was going to be an extra-long night.

Henry, her saddlebags thrown over her shoulder and her clothes showing the trials of the trail, stood in front of the high desk and asked quietly for a room. The hotel's middle-aged female owner wearing a stylish dress peered down her long nose at Henry who realized how disreputable she must appear to the woman in front of her. The woman noted Henry's lack of luggage and clearly less than pristine condition saying quite emphatically, "This establishment does not rent rooms to single women."

A male voice sounded from behind Henry.

"Well, that's just why my wife and I picked this place to stay. We'll need a couple of baths with that room, ma'am," Tanner said as he set his saddlebags down on the floor and took out a few coins to pay for the room in advance.

The matron gazed into Tanner's blue eyes, saw the grin on his face, and melted. "Of course, sir. How long do you think you and the Missus will be with us?" She turned the registry book so Tanner could sign.

After the formalities had been dealt with, Tanner picked up his bags and rifle and motioned for Henry to precede him up the stairs to their room. Henry didn't say anything, not even to give a piece of her mind to him about butting into her affairs which proved how really tired she was.

"You take the first bath while I scope out the town a little. Half an hour work for you?" he asked giving her some privacy to get cleaned up and feel more alive.

"Yes, that should be fine. I need to get about a pound of grit out of my hair and my mouth," she said as she searched through her bag for soap and clean clothes.

"Take your time then. I'll try to find a good place to eat this late." He went out, closing the door behind him.

The bathing room was clean, and there were towels available for the guest's use. Henry turned on the tap and felt the hot water come out of the spigot immediately. Undressing, she stepped into the tub, the abundance of hot water making her almost giddy. She ducked her head and lathered it, repeating the lathering and luxuriating in a full rinse.

Feeling two pounds lighter, she leaned back and let the water ease the muscles on her lower back and thighs. She certainly wasn't used to doing this much riding and wondered at some people's ability to ride for days and not fold up as soon as they dismounted.

This warm relaxing water was making her drowsy and in that half-awake half-asleep state, she thought about Tanner although she knew she shouldn't. She had been trying to distance herself from him at least physically ever since Madam Lillian implied Henry may be missing out on happiness by denying her attraction to Tanner.

And that bothered Henry. Was she really still punishing herself for not being able to save Martin? Was she setting herself above God in thinking she could decide who should die and who should be saved?

She knew she kept a distance from the people she met both in town and on the ranches in her adopted home. At first, she convinced herself it was because she wasn't sure she was staying in the little town, but she had been there three years now. One of the most attractive things about the place was that no one knew about her inability to save Martin.

No one knew how the overwrought parents had blamed her and her lack of knowledge as the reason their son died. And her own guilt never let her forget their accusations and the fact that there might have been some half-truths to their blame.

After going over the boy's symptoms and his death, Henry knew she hadn't missed anything. He would have still died, probably sooner without her intervention, but she had come up with this same conclusion before. Only this time she felt as if maybe she could forgive herself a little bit. Allow that she wasn't to blame as much as impotent to save him. No human could set themselves above God and His plans.

Talking over the event with Tanner in the dark, hearing the words out loud brought it all back to her, but it also seemed to act as a catharsis. Tanner never showed doubt she had done her best since she told him she had. She needed to forgive herself or she would never have peace or the happiness that would only be available when she accepted her limitations.

Henry was dressed when Tanner returned to the hotel room. She had rinsed out her shirtwaists and camisole in the tub and was trying to find a good drying place for them. His gaze swept over the wet clothing then to her and smiled.

"I do believe this is the first time on this trip I've seen you in regular street clothes, Ma'am. May I make your acquaintance?" he teased seeing the matching shirtwaist and skirt with the double flounces around the hem and the lace at the collar and cuffs of the shirtwaist.

"It's not too badly wrinkled considering how long it's been rolled up. I don't have any other hat though," she told him, her hair braided and wrapped on top of her head.

"No silk flowers or brooch in that bottomless saddlebag of yours?" he said still teasing her.

"No, well, wait." She dug around a little and pulled out a cloth flower corsage that went at the collar of a shawl which she pulled out, too. She pinned the flowers into her hair and turned and smiled at Tanner as he nodded his agreement.

"Looks right pretty. If you can wait a few minutes for your meal while I get cleaned up some… I ran across a restaurant I think will make you very happy. And I found out there isn't any brothels here, too small of a town. They just have a few girls over at the saloon." Grabbing his saddlebag, he left her to take his bath.

Henry didn't want to know how he found information so quickly, probably some kind of special service among single men new to town. When Tanner came back, all spruced up, they both stared at the one bed and faced the fact one of them was going to continue to sleep on the hard floor. Or they could take turns using the bed since they weren't going to be there many days any way this turned out. They would leave and follow the revival tent when it left if they hadn't found a way to charge the reverend with any crime.

Henry broached the subject rationally. "We sleep within feet of each other all the nights on the trail so we can handle this. I'll sleep under the sheet and you sleep on top and back to back. Does that work for you, Tanner?" She tried to keep her voice from wavering or showing doubt. This wasn't any different than being on bedrolls next to one another, and they've been doing that for several days now.

"Yep, that seems fair by me."

At dinner, Henry could see a poster advertising the tent revival and the Reverend Agape. Her mind was whirling, trying to think of a way to stop this man, have Mary be the last victim. Then it came to her, the perfect method to catch and arrest the minister.

"Tanner, I've got it. We won't have to follow the reverend but have him come to us."

Tanner stopped eating and looked up from his dinner warily.

"So," Henry continued when she knew she had his attention, "I resemble those dead women who attracted the reverend or whoever it is travelling with the revival show that is killing them. I mean my hair is reddish, and I'm small like they were. I can go and mix with the saloon girls here and try to draw his attention. That means I probably shouldn't be seen with you tonight when you visit the tent. You can study the men there better without me, anyways."

Tanner's brows drew down. "I don't like it."

"You don't like it because the idea was mine. If you had thought of it, you'd be all excited," she accused.

"Let me think about it a minute. My first reaction is to protect you. After all, you're not a Ranger. You didn't volunteer to put yourself in danger. You were just supposed to tell us if Lucy was poisoned or took her own life. This is getting a little out of control."

She could see he wasn't impressed with her idea, with allowing her to get close to the man they were sure killed at least three maybe as many as five young women. All of them prostitutes and all of them killed in the rooms they made their livelihood in. She could understand his hesitancy, but how else were they going to lure the man into the open and apprehend him in the act of committing a crime?

"I won't be in danger. You'll be right there with me watching for Agape to make his move. I'll never be alone with him, and I certainly won't eat or drink anything. Nothing bad can happen to me, and we have the chance of ending this man's killing spree."

She could see he was thinking, not throwing out the idea completely. "After tomorrow night, he'll be moving on to another city and it's much larger than this one, probably having multiple saloons and other places to watch over. We can't be everywhere at once so if we can't follow the reverend or he's not the one then we lost the chance to catch the killer and another innocent woman may lose her life," argued Henry, telling Tanner everything she had already gone over in her mind.

He began to nod. "I agree. I think catching him in the act will be the best method to get a conviction, but I don't want to hang you out there like bear bait. I'll see what the Major thinks, and we'll go and talk to the owner of the saloon or whoever's in charge of the girls there. We'll have to get him on our side, to allow you to mingle with the working girls. And you're right. I'll stay by your side so you won't be man-handled by any of the men."

"Won't that defeat the purpose of me being there? If I'm not available how will he get at me? Won't the preacher simply select an easier target?"

"Either follow my rules or it won't be happening. That's the only way you'll be there at all, and the Major will agree with me when I explain the plan in the wire."

CHAPTER FIVE

Major Withers was in town by early morning and going with Tanner to the saloon, Henry right on their heels. They were the only ones in the bar with the morning rays showing off the dirty windows and dusty chandeliers. The floor was still littered with last night's debris, and the Major, a big man with bushy gray mustache, called out for the owner of the establishment.

A large rather forceful woman called out from an upstairs room that she would be right down. A few minutes later the older, bleached-blonde woman, her hairpiece a little eschewed, came down the stairs, trying to make a gracious entrance for the three people waiting next to the bar.

"I'm the patroness here, name's Mel. Gentlemen, Ma'am, how can I be of service?" Her gaze roved over the Major's body a little longer than needed.

Tanner allowed the Major to take the lead on explaining why they were in town and their plan for catching the man responsible. He finished by saying, "We think the ladies who work here may be in danger from this murderer. There's been a dead body in the last few towns, and I'd hate there to be another." The Major's expression seemed to make the woman think he was personally worried for her safety.

"Why, Major, I appreciate your consideration, but

we can protect ourselves. I have the bartender and a bouncer who can take care of any man trying to harm one of my, ah, one of the ladies working here. I do thank you for the warning, though." She fluttered her lashes at the Major, giving him a shy smile. It was difficult a woman this experienced could appear shy, but she did. Must be an art at her age.

Henry couldn't hold back seeing her plan being lost and the possibility of catching the culprit postponed. "Really, Mel, the others had that same type of protection, but this killer isn't going to come right out and attack the girl. He lures her to him, he gets her to trust him, then he secretly, silently poisons her. When she's found, it appears to be a suicide and that the woman died in her sleep, but it was anything besides a serene death. I assure you the victim dies painfully and with knowledge she's been poisoned."

Now having the woman's full attention, Henry continued, "The poison first starts as little pains like needle pricks in her stomach followed by wrenching pain that has her writhing on the floor, foaming at the lips, sometimes causing blood to ooze from her nose and mouth before finally drowning in her own vomit. It isn't a pretty sight, and no one should end their life like that."

The older woman's eyes had become round as she put her hand to her own mouth saying, "I've seen women who've taken poison and they looked like they'd gone through hell. I didn't realize it was so painful, too." Mel seemed to be remembering the suicides she had evidently witnessed. She came to a decision. "I'll do it. I'll let you mix with the girls, and I'll tell them you're new and just joining us. No one

61

will know you're not one of us, but me."

"You won't be sorry, I promise. Do you have any redheads? Any gingers on, ah, staff? I want to attract him to me, so we need to take out the competition. We'll pay for anything they would have made tonight, including your commission." Henry noted the Major's head nodding in agreement.

The older lady nodded her head as well saying, "I can do that. I have two, and they're young and small, too. I'll make sure they keep out of sight, and you can wear some of their things if you don't have anything appropriate."

It seemed odd for the madam to consider the clothes Henry was wearing not appropriate since they covered her completely. But that was probably the problem and Henry accepted, saying, "I would appreciate that, and if you have any tips as to how I should behave I would appreciate the knowledge. I don't want to do anything that would warn him I'm not what I seem."

Henry felt Tanner tense beside her as the blonde merely laughed saying, "Oh, women instinctively know how to behave to make a man interested, but I'll give you a few pointers. Being young and pretty are two of the many aphrodisiacs, and you already have those."

The madam laughed at Tanner's astonished expression.

Henry, Tanner, and the Major left to discuss the finer points of the trap back in the hotel. Tanner knew he was being unusually quiet, and finally the Major suggested Henry go to her room in case someone was in town from the revival and spotted her there with the two Rangers. Henry said she would go back to the saloon instead and begin her acting part, staying in character while she was there.

Once she was gone, the Major faced Tanner across the table in the hotel's lobby and said quietly, "I don't usually get involved in a man's private life, but this is kind of a work situation, too. After all, I was the one who sent you after Henry, but I never thought you were one to mess where you live. I think highly of the girl, and she isn't set up to get caught in a one or two-night fling."

The older man stopped and watched as Tanner felt his cheeks burn, embarrassed to be taken to task by his superior.

The Major's lips firmed before continuing, "You know what I mean, Tanner. She's not very worldly, even though she is well aware of the world's dangers. That doesn't save her from men like you."

"I haven't stepped out of line, Sir, not once. But if she is open to something, I can't say that you or anyone else has the right to tell me not to accept her offer," Tanner told his superior officer bravely. He felt he needed to be honest with the man as well as with himself. Once this assignment was over, he knew he would approach Henry as a man to a woman. Ask to spend more time with her. Ask her to give him a chance.

"You're a Ranger and you're on assignment so you need to remember how you present yourself is how the Rangers will be represented. I know being on this case has probably tested your patience and endurance, but you're strong enough to keep your distance from her for another day or two."

His commanding officer looked at him sternly.

"I'm sending her home after tonight. I never meant for her to get this involved, and now she's being put in a dangerous position. But I don't see a faster way of capturing this man and getting him locked up and hanged."

"I'll never take advantage of her, Sir. But I admit she has some kind of draw on me. I really like her as a person, not just a woman. It's a little different for me, but I like the feeling," admitted Tanner.

"Then like it on your own time." They stood to go their separate ways. "Maybe you're finally growing up, Tanner. Nice to see it."

Tanner wished he could be near Henry to watch over her and make sure she was all right in implementing their plan.

The night before he had gritted his teeth hoping he didn't do something to embarrass himself with her while he was sleeping. Since he never was one to cuddle, he felt they may be all right for a day or two. Wanting to keep her safe may have escalated his need to keep her close. Maybe the Major was correct in telling him to ignore the attraction and keep to getting the job done. After all, Henry had never made any signs she was attracted to him, so it was all on his side. Once he took her home, this would all be over and he would return to his station and wait for another assignment.

The madam, Mel, introduced Henry to the other ladies as they finally woke up and mingled in the upstairs parlor area. They arrived one by one, many wearing sleeping clothes which were basically under garments. Some showed interest in the new woman in their midst while others appeared bored, yawning and stretching as they lounged on the sofas and upholstered chairs.

The room wasn't as nice as Miss Lillian's brothel, but it was relatively clean and decorated to meet the client's needs and taste for luxury. There were tassels on the velvet curtains and gilt framed oils of nudes and Greek mythology. Fringed pillows and patterned rugs on the scuffed wood floor. Enough for a local cowhand to feel he was being taken care of, Henry was sure.

"This here is...." Then she stopped so Henry could fill in the gap, which the other ladies didn't seem odd.

"Henrietta," added Henry.

Mel rolled her eyes and finished, "This here is, Etta. She's new as you see and is joining us but will need a little of our help to be ready by tonight." Which announcement made all of them stand and come closer talking over one another, each having their own ideas of what needed to be primped or padded, tweezed or shaved.

It was the first time in her life Henry was ever frightened since these women meant business. They picked up her hair appreciating its softness, color, and shine asking her what soap she used. Then Mel held Henry's chin between her fingers and turned her this way and that as they discussed a hairstyle to best set off her fine features. Some girls who left returned with a rather concealing dress, considering what they were wearing, although it was much more daring than anything Henry had ever worn before.

"I think since she's new and young, she should play the ingénue," said the woman named Bess.

"I agree," said another as they seemed to nod as one, and Henry turned to Mel for an explanation.

Mel was happy to inform her saying, "Act virginal, you know like you have no idea of what the men are here for. Flirt, even talk a little naughty. That will have 'em hanging their tongues out."

Henry was hoping Mel remembered Henry was just here to catch a killer, not entertain some man. Acting like a virgin wasn't going to be a hard stretch. Other than she understood what occurred in reproduction and that it was very pleasant, for the male at least, she had no experience with men. Tanner being the only man she spent any time with other than her classmates, who had all been too busy studying to worry about anything else.

A pretty, full figured girl came toward Henry with wicked looking tweezers saying, "Here, Dearie, put some of this petroleum jelly on your eyebrows and it won't hurt as much."

Another girl a little older laughed, saying, "Tell the poor girl where else she should put that so it won't hurt as much." Which statement had most of the others whooping in laughter.

Henry tried not to blush, but said, "I think I understand, but I don't think that will be necessary."

"Oh, a real professional, are you? Well, most of the men that come here are cheap S.O.B.s and will tie a string around their Johnsons to make sure they get their full hours' worth." This brought more raucous laughter as they worked together to ready Henry for the night to come.

Mel, laughing with the others, said, "Now ladies, you're going to scare our new member off if you keep talking like that." Then turning to Henry, told her, "Don't worry, Honey, I'm sure you'll draw the gentlemen, being as refined as you are. It's a good role to hold on to."

"Until a guy's been in your bed a few dozen times. He tends to catch on by then," said the girl called Sarah.

Henry knew she didn't have to face that future and felt a little sorry for these women even if they seemed accepting of their way of life and had formed a sort of society within their limited lifestyle.

After two hours, Henry stared at a stranger in the mirror in front of her. She was wearing an evening dress that showed off her creamy shoulders as well as a wide expanse of skin above her breasts, the cleavage in full sight of anyone taller than she was, and that meant just about everyone.

The dress was tight to her narrow waist then flared out with a number of crinolines and several rows of lace in wider bands around the hemline. There was also a full bustle, the cloth cascading like a waterfall that made sitting difficult, forcing the wearer to stand so the silhouette could be admired.

Her hands and arms appeared delicate and very lady-like, pale and smooth. But the biggest change was with her face. She knew her eyes were one of her best features, but with a little bit of tweezing, they now looked huge and doe like. The lashes having been darkened with charcoal and more of the petroleum jelly. But first, they had patted rice powder on her face, adding color back with rouge and reddened her lips with more rouge emphasizing her cupid shaped mouth.

Pulling her hair back on each side leaving fat ringlets to frame her face. The major portion was left to hang down her back in even more ringlets, like a very young girl. In fact, she seemed much younger, rather than older, with the make-up and realized why Mel suggested the act that Henry follow.

Henry had been offered dinner, but her stomach was too tight with excitement, and something she couldn't name, to eat. She was anxious to see Tanner's reaction to her change in appearance and, of course, having the Reverend Agape pointed out to her so she could try to lure him into giving himself away. She looked forward to the Rangers arresting him. Ridding the world of the danger to young women like those who helped her get ready this evening.

She knew the Major was to be in the saloon but wasn't sure if there were any other Rangers with him. She hoped there were. She would feel better if there was more than the two men to apprehend this killer. Henry felt Agape would run as soon as he felt in danger of getting caught.

Mel came back into the parlor saying, "Men are arriving, and the rest of the girls have gone down. I saw your man there, and he's trying to look calm, but I've seen men walking up the gallows' steps easier of mind."

"Tanner didn't want me to do this, not really, although he knew better than to try to prevent me. He just set up some ground rules," explained Henry as she followed Mel out and to the top of the stairs not misunderstanding who Mel had been referring to as 'your man'.

Approaching the stairs, Henry could hear the talking and women's laughter as well as the clinking of glassware and scuffing of boots and chairs across the worn wood floor. Just as Henry appeared at the top of the stairs and was about to descend, a quiet came over the room below. Mel smiled widely, apparently taking the awe as sign she and her ladies did an outstanding job dressing Henry. Unsure the quiet was due to her arrival, Henry continued to descend to the main floor.

Tanner practically jumped from his place at the bar to the bottom of the stairs, smiling as he put out his hand and took possession of Henry. He let the other men showing interest know they were no longer competition as he seemingly dismissed them from his world. Tanner felt a little dazed. But he didn't say anything to give Henry away or that they knew each other, instead, added to the show by taking her to the bar and ordering her a drink.

Tanner smiled. "You new to town, miss?" Tanner asked sweeping his gaze over her from head to hem, letting his pleasure at her changes show on his face.

"Ye-yes, I am. Are you a local or just passing through?" she asked and took a sip of the drink the bartended set in front of her. "Mel told me to order champagne when a man offered to buy me a drink. This is the first time I've ever had it, and I like it."

"I may stay around a little while now that I've met you. Name's Tanner." He tipped his hat to her as he watched the men's expressions around them. They hadn't thought this through very well because every face he saw had avarice in his eyes, coveting Henry as she stood there so beautiful and youthful, sweet yet alluring, ready to be awoken to the delights of her very attractive body. Too classy for a place like this.

Then Tanner caught sight of the Major with his eyes half-closed as if the smoke from the cheroot he was smoking was irritating them. Snapping into full Ranger manner, Tanner stopped staring at Henry and all the possibilities between them. He began to search for

69

the reverend he saw last night preaching of hell and brimstone for sinners. He found him, sitting off in the far corner, and the man's gaze was riveted on Henry.

Tanner touched his glass to Henry's in a salute and to fend off the man on her other side who finally had built up enough lust to speak with her even though Tanner was in possession. Tanner pulled her out onto the dance floor when the piano began "The Yellow Rose of Texas".

Again, all eyes seemed to be on Henry, but Tanner had his arm around her, and if he kept moving he could keep her out of anyone else's. She may be bait, but she wasn't supposed to be eaten alive in the process.

He thought, for sure, she would be the same woman who accompanied him all along the trail, but to find this elegant, beautiful woman in his arms was causing him all sorts of physical problems. She was the same yet more. More womanly and more attractive to him. He fought the urge to take her out the swing doors and disappear with her until he could satisfy his other needs she brought to the surface.

He knew he would have to give her up eventually especially since Agape was already here just as they had hoped. He needed to put Henry in the rotter's reach and then watch like a hawk for any sign he was going to harm her.

Swinging Henry in his arms was rewarding, but he knew their time together was limited. In more ways than one. Soon the Rangers would have their man and Henry would be sent home, miles from him, and if he knew his commanding officer, miles from Tanner's next assignment.

Henry felt as if she was in heaven. She was a

princess and Tanner was her Prince Charming, being held in his arms and danced around the mostly empty dance floor. The faces blurred, but most of the other people were having a good time. She could still hear talking and laughing and the lively piano which was played with gusto if not finesse.

Tanner leaned down and whispered in her ear, "The reverend's here, in that corner, clean shaven, wearing all black except his shirt, but without the cleric's collar. He's been watching you, so I think we have our man. Just have to get him to do something to incriminate himself."

Then Henry laughed and slapped him lightly on the shoulder as if he had said something naughty to her and that she had enjoyed it. Tanner seemed amazed at her ability to act.

The music turned into a love song as Mel, wearing an evening gown that could have been seen at the opera in New York, sang. Most everyone's attention was drawn to the piano and the large woman there. Tanner and Henry were under the stairs near the storeroom door when they stopped, and both took a moment to rest.

Henry peered up and met Tanner's gaze and all sound disappeared, no more singing or laughter or piano notes. The brightly lit room faded and there was only the two of them as they were drawn to one another by some unseen force, like a magnet until his lips covered hers and Henry had her first grown-up kiss.

It only lasted a moment, but when Tanner pulled back and stood straighter the light and noise and piano all returned in an unwanted roar, as if they were dropped into some kind of hole with all these other people.

Henry knew Tanner felt the same way. She was sure of it as she touched her lips in awe.

"Don't worry, Henry, your make-up is still perfect. I'm sorry. I should have waited to do that," he apologized.

Staring shyly into his shirt, she said, "I really should make myself more available to the reverend. Lure him into trying something."

Tanner's hand tightened a little on her elbow, but then he agreed. "You're right. I admit I can't completely monopolize you or this whole night will be for naught. I'll stay close. Just play with that chain around your neck if you need me and I'll be at your side before you know."

Making his way to the bar, Tanner watched covertly as she made her way to the table the preacher occupied.

Henry nodded, feeling bereft after he left her to stand next to the bar and order another drink as she made her way to Agape. The reverend's eyes watched avidly as she moved toward the man. Several men tried to approach and although Henry was friendly, she made it known she wasn't ready to go upstairs just yet. That seemed to confuse the men, but they accepted her answer and faded back into the growing crowd.

It was becoming busier, and it was difficult to see across the room, there were so many people dancing now. The piano plunked out its form of music, the talking and laughter all getting louder, each trying to drown the other out, trying to take precedence.

But Tanner was always watching even when it appeared he had forgotten her. She would catch him watching her reflection in the big mirror behind the bar, nursing a mug of warm beer. He made no sign he saw her, but she took comfort in the fact and decided to take the bull by the horns.

The preacher was sitting alone in the noisy, bustling establishment and not paying attention to anyone except Henry. He didn't look dangerous or much like a preacher either without a cleric collar or even a tie. He looked like a man out for a good time, even if he wasn't smiling. Many of the men in the bar seemed to take their evening entertainments seriously.

His mousy brown hair and brown eyes wouldn't send a maiden's heart to palpitations, but there was something in his gaze. Something that even Henry, knowing his particulars, could still be drawn to if she hadn't been forewarned. That must be what kept people coming to his tent night after night when he was in a town. Some sort of message he sent out that others wanted to be a part of.

Walking past the reverend, she would respond to his slightest movement as an invitation to stop and speak with him. As she thought, the preacher was watching her progress and as soon as she was near the table he adopted as his own, he lifted the glass in front of him in salute and Henry responded immediately.

"Could I get you another, sir?" she asked, smiling, and peeked down coyly, pretending that meeting his gaze was more than a shy girl like herself could manage.

"No, it's just water, but if you don't mind, I could use some company," he said politely.

"Certainly, I'm tired of standing, and you seem like you need someone to talk to," she said again keeping her smile pasted to her lips.

"I talk all day. It would be nice to sit and listen for a while. Do you like working here? Are the other girls nice?" he asked. Henry wasn't sure where this was going so answered thinking this was how he lured the young women. Asking innocent questions and lowering their defenses. She would play along.

"I'm new here, but they've all been nice so far," Henry said honestly, in case he had spoken with one of the other girls. "I think I'll like it here though. The town is nice and clean."

"Do you think you'd like to change? Maybe get married and have a family? I'd be good to you, and my other wives are getting older. A young wife like you would be able to help the sister-wives with a lot of the heavier work." He smiled as if this were the most normal of conversations.

"I, ah, I've never thought about it." Then she improvised, "Women like me don't get many real proposals of marriage."

"Well, this is a real proposal, but, of course, you will give up consorting, drinking, cussing, and using the Lord's name in vain. I will not tolerate impure behavior near my children and sister-wives," he stated firmly.

"You have children?" She tried not to let her voice squeak but lost the battle.

He replied, "Yes, seventeen, so you see my need for another wife."

Henry didn't actually. It sounded like he needed anything, but a wife. Perhaps some Goodyear condoms, but not another wife to impregnate.

"I see," was all Henry could say not wanting to offend the man.

"Sisters Rebecca and Rachel do their best which makes them very busy, too busy for wifely duties, and I recently lost my third wife, Sister Bethany. Someone like yourself, used to those duties has a great appeal to me."

He peered at Henry lustily, leaving her no doubt his desires were well kindled merely talking with her. She knew he bedded Mary if not Lucy, but she didn't want to put herself into the position of being alone with him knowing what happened to the other women who fell for his lonely man routine.

Unconsciously, Henry began playing with her necklace and she saw Tanner on his way across the room. When the Reverend Agape saw him approaching, he blanched and got up so quickly he tipped the small table onto Henry, taking her down roughly to the floor.

The preacher ran, trying to escape through the side door into the attached hotel lobby. There was a commotion as the Major, dressed as a miner with a big slouched hat pulled low over his face, took off after him. At least one other man besides Tanner chased after the disappearing man.

Henry had to catch her breath while strong feminine hands helped her upright and pulled her out of the way as other patrons set the table on its legs and the chair Henry had been seated on upright. Henry went unresisting with the person helping her up and away from the turmoil. Many of the customers were talking with each other about what they saw and heard or thought was occurring.

Henry turned thanking the woman who helped her and found it wasn't one of the girls as she expected, but an older woman with her graying hair pulled back in a tight bun covered with a white muslin cap, her dark dress free of any button or trim.

"Thank you, ah, may I have your name so I know to whom I'm speaking?" Henry asked.

"Of course, I'm Sister Rebecca, Brother Ambrose's first wife. I'm here because my husband has shown a distinct interest in you, and I must vet you to see if you are an appropriate woman to become a member of our family. After all, there are many children to be concerned with, and your values will need to agree with ours or it simply will not work. Brother Ambrose has been disappointed before," the woman told Henry, and Henry listened wondering if there wasn't more to this woman's helping Henry up.

The men sitting close to the two women were watching them curiously and Sister Rebecca said, "Can we go somewhere less public where there are not men staring at me with such lust?"

Henry was about to tell the woman she had nothing to worry about, but then thought that would be rude and agreed to go upstairs so they could talk in the parlor. Henry was sure this woman could help get the evidence against her husband if she were asked the right questions.

Once upstairs, the women faced one another and Henry noticed the woman's pupils were very dilated and her breathing somewhat erratic, even considering they had just climbed a set of stairs.

"Ah, Mrs., I mean, Sister Rebecca, I think you misunderstand any relationship between your husband and myself. But I would like to speak with you..." Henry began, but was interrupted by the woman.

"No, I must ask you about your beliefs and if you

can find it in yourself, deep in your soul, to give up fornication and sin. If you can pledge yourself to Brother Ambrose and his promise to travel this country bringing the name of the Lord to those who have given up on Him? To keep yourself only for His use and to promise to follow our ways of life. Do you promise all these things?" By now the older woman's voice was raised, her eyes appeared glassy and wild, and Henry was frightened of her.

"I, I think I can do that. Is that what you want, what Brother Ambrose wants?" Henry asked, realizing leaving the crowded saloon might have been a mistake, hopefully not one that would cost Henry her life. She hoped one of the other girls would bring a customer up the stairs soon and past the archway, anyone to stop in to find out why she and this woman were in there.

"I do not have a voice in the matter other than to make sure you will stay loyal to Brother Ambrose and his preaching. The fact you will be taking over my position in his affections does not sway my ruling one way or the other. You must go through the purification and then we can find Brother Ambrose and let him know you have passed the tests put to you."

Henry saw her take a small glass vial with a cork stopper out of a hidden pocket in her skirt. That's when Henry realized it wasn't the reverend they should have been watching, but this wife. The wife was mentally unstable, and their lifestyle and her husband's constant search for a younger woman, though less pure, was driving her mad. But it was who he wanted to warm his bed. Not the loyal woman who had probably borne him many of those seventeen children.

"Sister Rebecca, I think we need to talk more. I

have decided my life ways would not be good for your family, that the children might be better off without me being involved. Please give Brother Ambrose my answer," Henry said hoping to get the woman to leave so she could find Tanner or the Major and tell him what had occurred.

"No, you must go through the purification rites. Brother Ambrose will return and bed you, and you must be made pure before that. Come here and kneel down so I may anoint you with the oil of cloves, and you will feel clean and as innocent as a newborn," the insane woman said holding out her arms as Henry had seen some statues of the Virgin Mary posed.

Henry stayed in place, not sure what the poison was. Getting too close could allow the older woman to splash it onto Henry's skin or eyes causing the same death throes as drinking it would.

"I don't want this, and I'm leaving." Henry turned to leave, and that's when the woman pulled out a Reed palm-sized gun. The small derringer style, single bullet gun wasn't known to be very accurate except at this close range, so Henry stopped in mid-step.

"Now I see you understand I will do anything to make Brother Ambrose happy. You will go through the purification and then become a sister-wife if you pass," Rebecca stated.

Henry decided to take the woman's views straight on. "You mean if I live through a poisoning?"

At the woman's startled expression, Henry continued, "You have poisoned all the women who Ambrose has found attractive for I don't know how long. You don't want to share his affections or his body, especially with the kind of women who he has been trying to bring into your family. Not after you and Rachel have dedicated your lives to him and his causes. And there was the wife who died and…"

At the older woman's startled movement, Henry continued, "Oh, you had something to do with that, too, didn't you? One of your sister-wives take more than her fair share of Ambrose's time?"

"You know nothing of our life. Sister Bethany should have remained pure of thought, but instead she bragged about how much and how often Brother Ambrose visited her bed. Just because I've gotten too old to conceive does not mean it would be impossible. We could have had a miracle child. In the Bible, Sarah had a son of Abraham when she was ninety years old."

The woman had tears in her eyes, and her mouth trembled. "I'm half that, and yet Brother Ambrose said I was too old and it was time to get another younger wife. I was to help him. I was to make sure she was a woman who could live his life with him. So far, there has been no one suitable." Rebecca seemed righteous in her anger.

"But I don't want to belong to Ambrose or to your family. I'm sorry, but I love another, and I'll go to him immediately if I receive your permission to leave," Henry told the woman honestly, trying to reason with an unreasonable person.

Rebecca appeared confused, not knowing what to do. Henry figured the older woman had probably never faced this dilemma before. She was convinced any woman would jump at a chance to join with Ambrose just to get out of the brothel they lived in. With Henry assuring Sister Rebecca she didn't want Ambrose, how was Rebecca going to proceed?

"Henry, we've got..." Tanner had reached the doorway, stopping abruptly at seeing the small gun pointed at Henry.

Henry smiled, saying pleasantly, "Why here's my man now. I was just telling Sister Rebecca, first wife of Brother Ambrose, that you and I had an understanding. I wasn't, in fact, available to marry the good reverend."

"That's right, this is my fiancée," he told the older woman, who had turned pale at his appearance.

"I don't understand, don't you work here?" Sister Rebecca asked Henry.

"No, I'm a veterinarian and I only danced with Tanner."

Henry could see this truth worried Rebecca. The older woman seemed to be trying to rationalize what she had done to the other young women and evidently finding holes in her own thinking.

"I, I don't understand. I thought for sure Ambrose wanted you," she said letting her hand holding the gun drop to her side.

Henry knew Tanner was taking his weight onto one foot so he could spring at the woman, but it wouldn't keep Rebecca from shooting. Whether she shot at him or Henry was up for debate.

"But she isn't available as we both just told you. I think maybe you should come with me to see Ambrose. We've got him in the sheriff's office, and he's kind of confused as to what we're talking about, so maybe you can explain," Tanner said quietly as Rebecca became more and more agitated.

The disturbed woman began to shake her head in a negative manner, saying, "They were impure...not pure, not pure enough to be Brother Ambrose's wife."

With a wild look in her eyes, she lifted her left hand pouring the liquid into her mouth, gagging a little before forcing it down.

"No!" Henry and Tanner yelled, but both were too late to prevent the woman from swallowing.

The inevitable happened. Dropping to the floor, the older woman clutched her stomach, curling into a fetal position. Foam formed at her mouth, her body spasming while trying to retch, but her mind refusing to allow it. She writhed and twitched. Then there was nothing.

Tanner grabbed Henry and held her tightly. "I can't believe we were so set on it being a man. I almost lost you. I thought Ambrose was the one and we were down there sweating him, and you were up here facing the real killer. I'm so sorry, Henry, I'll never leave you alone again."

"I'm all right. Don't expect more from yourself than all you can do. I went upstairs with her and never felt in danger until she became unstable. I've never faced a person so alienated from her own mind. I never had training as an alienist." She laughed then hiccupped as tears came streaming down her face.

"Oh, Henry, darlin', don't cry. You're never going to be in this kind of a situation again. I'll never let anything bad happen to you, I promise." Tanner spoke into her hair as he held her tightly to his chest. She convulsed in tears until she had no more tears to cry.

The Major came in on a run, stopping short just as Tanner had. "Ambrose said something that made me think he really didn't know what was going on, but I see you two figured out the same thing only sooner." He went over to the woman and looked down without pity.

Tanner explained while keeping Henry held close, "I'm not sure why she was doing it, but this is the killer. Henry would have been another victim except I came back because I couldn't figure out why she wasn't right behind us. She's not one to let someone else finish her job."

She noted he ignored his commanding officer's expression of concern as the Major took note of their entwined arms.

"Let me go so I can change out of these clothes," Henry said as she stood back and faced the Major. "I think I want to return to my room if you don't need me anymore tonight. I'll write out what happened tomorrow if that helps."

"You've done a good job and have been very brave. I never meant for you to get this involved, Henry, but we got the killer, and Texas owes you a debt of gratitude," the Major told her. "I'll have Tanner escort you back to your hotel room. Then I'll see to getting you home no matter what, tomorrow."

"Thank you, I really wanted to help, and I'm glad no one got hurt." Henry stared down at the dead woman, her eyes rolled up into her head and finished, "Well, no one who didn't bring it on themselves, that is."

CHAPTER SIX

Changing into her own clothes, Henry wiped the makeup off with some face cream she found in Mel's room. She left a brief note of thanks for the woman and short explanation, but she figured the Major would fill in the saloon owner and possibly stay for a celebratory drink with her. Henry was pretty sure there was some mutual admiration going on between the two.

Tanner and Henry were quiet on the way to the hotel. They left by way of the back stairs to miss the crowded saloon which was still noisy and rowdy and full of life. No one realized what had happened upstairs, no one realized a life was lost while many more saved.

When they entered the hotel room, Henry said, "Leave the lamp off. I don't want to face the light again tonight. The darkness seems softer, safer somehow."

"I understand, let me help you though. You've had a shock, and maybe I should go and get a bottle or something to help you sleep," Tanner offered as she removed her hat and he sat her down to remove her shoes, rubbing her feet between his large hands.

"I know what will help me sleep," she murmured suggestively.

His hands stopped moving, his breath held as he waited her pronouncement.

"You. I need you to help me get to sleep, to forget

all the death and the fear and the broken woman who loved too much and trusted too little."

"From what I've seen she seemed unbalanced to me. You can't blame her husband for that," he said reasonably, ignoring her invitation, giving her time to rescind it.

"I don't. She chose her life and how to live it, but she made me think. Am I living my life as I want, or was I pushed into a role I'm not suited to? Tonight, I felt beautiful and happy, even knowing I would be facing down a murderer. I enjoyed the freedom I found in the saloon as a working girl. I mean I loved the music and dancing with you, how you looked at me, the way you kissed me..." She placed her hands on his shoulders.

Tanner stood up from his kneeling position and pulled Henry up with him saying, "This is often a reaction after facing down death. You want to confirm you're alive. You want to validate your life by making love, and sometimes it's the worst thing you can do."

"Are you sure, Tanner, or are you afraid that what we have won't be as strong afterward?"

"I'm sure I want you so badly I'm strung as tight as cat gut in the sun, but I'm afraid I can't be what you need me to be. I'm afraid I'll let you down somehow, and I'd be angry at myself if you get hurt." Leaning down, he took the mouth she presented to him.

Then lifting her against his body, he said, "But I can't refuse what you're offering, darlin'. I'm going to accept your invitation if you really know what you're doing."

"I know what I'm doing, Tanner. I'm taking my chance with you. I'll worry about tomorrow,

tomorrow." She pulled his head down so she could return his kisses, so she could taste him as he was tasting her, his tongue plunging into her warm mouth in imitation of what he wanted to do with her body.

Tanner stroked her breast through the shirtwaist then tried to reach under it to her camisole. Frustrated, Henry quickly unbuttoned the top and threw it to the floor, followed by the camisole, giving him full access to her as she untied the waistband and stepped out of the ruffled skirt, leaving it on the floor.

Picking her up, Tanner carried her to the bed. Laying her down so his hands were free to remove his shirt by pulling it over his head. He yanked off his boots, hopping on one foot then the other. She heard him remove his trousers and Henry knew this was really going to happen. She was going to lie with Tanner, and she would always have this moment burned into her memory, whether with fond remembrances or regret was yet to be seen.

Tanner pushed Henry onto her back and covered her body with his as he again settled his mouth over hers and thrust his tongue in repeatedly. Soon he wasn't content with feeling her nipples harden against his palm, he needed to taste her there, too. He licked and suckled until Henry was writhing in need, arching up to his mouth to have him repeat his ministrations.

He kissed lower, finding the soft curls and sliding his tongue into her warmth, touching that responsive bud that had her lifting in the air, her hips trying to search out and find comfort from the feelings that were beginning to overwhelm her.

Tanner crawled back up her body, kissing and sucking along the way, his own need growing to a point he was having trouble containing it.

"Are you ready for me, darlin'? I'm so hot I don't think I can wait much longer."

"I want...I want you, too. Please, Tanner," she answered, thrashing her head back and forth, trying to assuage her building need for him which inflamed him more as he entered her, then felt her try to pull back, but it was too late. He penetrated and broke the maidenhead.

Henry held him close, her arms around his hips and her head pressed against his chest.

"I'm fine, please keep going...for me?" She almost begged, and Tanner was lost to all sense as he began the age-old rhythm to bring them both to culmination.

Relaxing, Henry felt the small glimmer of feeling that had fled with the pain reappear. It grew brighter and brighter until she splintered into a million fragments like a firework display on the Fourth of July, sprinkling little embers onto the fallow ground.

Tanner too met his peak and was breathing harshly into her ear. "I thought you said you knew what you were doing? I thought you meant you were experienced."

"Does it matter? Would you have said, no thank you, and gone on your way?" she asked him, still in the after-glow, knowing he would be honest with her.

He petted her hair out of her face confessing, "No, darlin', I think we were both past that point, but it's not to say I wouldn't have done things differently."

"I'd say you were down-right perfect." She kissed his chest, rubbing her nose in the soft hair there.

Hearing the smile in his voice, he replied, "Well, I thank you, ma'am. We Rangers tend to please."

"I was pleased, sir, I was very pleased." They fell asleep for the first time holding each other.

Henry woke with Tanner wrapped around her body as she lay on her side. His mouth was just at her ear as he kissed her cheek and covered a breast with his hand, playing with the sleepy nipple until it responded to his touch.

Henry, smiling with pleasure, asked, "Is this the way it always is? I thought you men needed time to rest in between."

"Darlin', no man needs that much time before he's rested enough. I was trying to be polite and let you sleep because I know you've been through a lot tonight already." He kneaded her breast and pushed his hips against her, penetrating her completely as he held her hips then fingered her most feminine part.

Henry again smiled and pushed back into him, making his few pushes seem puny. Tanner rolled her to face him, pulling her leg over his hip so he was poised at her entrance.

"You all right with this? You're not too sore or anything?" he asked, kissing her lips over and over.

"I'm fine, and I'm very much all right with this." She impaled herself on his shaft, tired of waiting for him to finish making love to her.

That was all Tanner needed to inflame him into giving her the best of him. What began as gentle lovemaking soon became him thrusting into her over and over, his large hands holding her in place.

He laid claim to her body until they both met a cataclysmic climax together, ending with them clutching one another to regain their breathing and balance. The two fell asleep again. Henry's leg thrown over Tanner's, the sheets entangled around them both.

The sun's rays were shining through the window they'd neglected to pull the shade down on. It was dark when they had gotten back to the room, and there were their other activities that took precedence over normal evening rituals.

"Mm-m-m-m, I love the way you smell, the feel of your hair against my chest, the feel of your skin against mine," Tanner said, and Henry felt what her naked body was doing to his as his erection pushed into her hip. "We can wake up every morning just like this. Well, every morning I'm not on assignment, that is, but I swear I'll hurry home to you to get more of you."

"What do you mean? Where will I be?" Henry asked not liking Tanner taking her for granted. After all, it's not as if they had an understanding or engagement.

"I'm not particular, but it should be closer to Austin than your farm is now. The Major is stationed there, and I work for him the most. I'm not stationed at any of the other cities," Tanner told her stroking her back down to her buttocks and up again.

"What am I supposed to do while you're gone? Take care of a house or something?" she asked not liking the description of the rest of her life. "Are you asking me to marry you?"

"Well, let's not rush into anything, darlin'." His hand stopped moving and Henry could hear panic enter his voice. "We've only known each other a few weeks, and marriage is a big step."

"Yes, marriage is a big step. You're right, we should think on it a little more. But right now, I need to get back home," Henry said as she searched for her camisole or shirtwaist, anything to cover her nakedness now daylight had brought back her common sense.

"Stay with me. Jason can take care of your house. We can have more time together before I get sent off on another assignment." Tanner stroked her arm, seeming to like the satiny feel of her skin under his calloused hand. "There's nothing you need to get back to, after all."

"I shouldn't have stayed," she said anxiously, realizing she hadn't thought past the lovemaking. "I should have left before, well, before we did what we…. I need to get home, get back to Richard and Jason and…" She tried to find something or someone who needed her more than she needed Tanner.

"Who the hell is Richard? You never mentioned there was another man. I don't trespass on another man's woman, so is that why you never mentioned him?" Tanner accused, sounding injured that she was involved with another man. As if it were she who changed in the middle of everything.

Henry watched with hurt eyes as Tanner distanced himself from her, turning and pulling on his trousers as if he couldn't get out of there fast enough.

"I didn't have to tell you the story of my whole life. We were only supposed to work on a case then I was to go back home. You've made it clear you weren't interested in anything more than that." Henry threw back at him thinking it unfair he got to push all the blame of what they did onto her, as if he wasn't an eager participant, as if she had seduced him against his will.

"You didn't tell me much, evidently. I expected

more of you, Henry. You know I was getting interested in you, and now you admit there's someone waiting for you to return home. I hope you're more honest with him. If he loves you, what we did last night won't matter. I just can't figure out why you didn't turn me away? It would have been easier if you had." He grabbed his hat and headed for the door.

"I don't know what came over me last night. It wasn't my usual behavior. I don't know why..." she said weakly as the door slammed behind him.

She sat on the bed, half-dressed and feeling...what? Part of her mind seemed numb and unable to think past the fact Tanner was out of her life, but could she get him out of her heart as easily? Last night was spectacular, and instead of making plans to merge their lives together they were going entirely separate directions.

Tanner's plan had been devised to meet his needs and wants, which Henry supposed was all right, but didn't she, shouldn't she, have some voice in what happens for the rest of her life? Maybe that was the problem. She was thinking forever, and Tanner was thinking what next.

She wasn't meant to be a rolling stone following Tanner as he moved around the state. It took months to build up confidence and trust in a community before ranchers and farmers would trust her to care for their animals. If she moved every year or even more often, she would never have a practice again.

But for her this wasn't about her career unlike it evidently was for Tanner. The problem was that after everything they'd been through, the long days talking and getting to know one another, he didn't know her well enough to know there wasn't a man in her life. He hadn't even given her a chance to explain. That was probably the death blow from the beginning.

It was almost as if he wanted to find something to drive them apart. Something or someone to blame for him leaving her after taking her virginity. He needn't have bothered. She was prepared to return to her life without him storming off and making up reasons to leave her.

Henry wasn't sure what happened except what they had done was the most wonderful event in her whole life, and she would cherish and abhor it at the same time. Outside her usual conduct, but one that couldn't be undone. Possibly with time she would forget Tanner and last night, but it will be a very long time off.

She thought about his warning, his asking if she was sure, and she thought she was, but that was before he started talking as if he owned her, had the right to tell her where to live. He wanted to change her life to meet his wants while forgetting she had a life, too.

He wasn't sure he wanted to make this permanent while she had made that commitment last night. What had she told him? Something about tomorrow, taking care of tomorrow? Well, now she saw the difference from moonlight and daylight. The daylight brought out the truth about feelings and fears and trust.

Tanner was a good Ranger, but a lousy man to get involved with. She knew it and for some reason, had pushed it back in her mind, wanting him to be the man she lay with, the man she would remember giving herself to the first time. She may be sorry for it right now, but as time passed, eventually she would revisit last night in her memory and not regret a thing.

Henry dressed in what she thought of as her city clothes and cowboy hat and packed her saddlebag then left to find out when the stage would head toward home. She would ride anything that got her out of this town and away from the thought of Tanner.

Skipping breakfast, she went to the livery where she made a fair deal to sell her horse and saddle. She liked the little mare, but the liveryman took good care of his animals and she was sure Guinevere would be happy there.

Taking that money, she found the stage office and bought a ticket on the stage due out in an hour. She left her saddlebags there to be put on the coach when it got in. It was a short lay-over, only long enough to drop off the mail and change horses.

Henry felt there was enough time to thank Mel and the other ladies for their help and to answer any questions. She walked down the street to the dim saloon.

There were several men at the bar and the tables. Evidently it wasn't too early in the day to drink. Mel wasn't there, but Tanner was, standing at the bar with a glass of whiskey in front of him. Henry should have guessed he would be here and turned to leave when she heard Tanner say something.

"What?" Henry said, not hearing Tanner's words.

"I asked if you was looking for a job," Tanner said, his stance one of a man asking for a fight.

"No, I am not, sir. I have a job. One I'm very attached to," she said, her back teeth tight together.

"Seems like the one you had last night might pay better. A good actress can be hard to find," he told her still not meeting her gaze.

"I find I can see much clearer in the daylight. Things that look good in the dark of night aren't quite so clean and straightforward in the light of day. Perhaps we both had blinders on. Seeing only straight ahead and not the whole of each other. I'm sorry if I misled you in any way, and I hope it would be the same with you. No one gains anything at this point in blaming one another. We were mistaken, that's all. It just happened." She turned and walked out of the swing doors.

Tanner stood there with his two hands on the wooden bar then yelled out, "Damn it, Henry, I love you." He looked around the suddenly silent saloon, noting the hard glare from many of the men and the curious looks from the women.

"Hell and damnation, Henry's a woman, so don't go gawking at me."

Some of the people went back to playing cards or drinking while others kept watching him as if he wasn't to be trusted.

Tanner told himself he'd never chase after a woman, and he wouldn't do so now. He'd wait a while, then on their way to his next assignment he would have time to explain his plans better. Marriage wasn't out of the question, just that he wasn't ready yet to make that commitment. Hell, that sounded lame even to him. He would have to make a better argument. They could reach a compromise he was sure.

He would drop Henry off in a safe town while he went on to Abilene, his next assignment, and help the marshal there, and then he would return to Henry. And then do what? Henry was right, there had to be a goal, an end to plan for.

It did seem lame in light of what he felt for her, but

he would convince her that what they felt for one another was better than anything this Richard could give her. Tanner might even give her that ring she seemed to think so important.

Downing his drink, he left the bar hating feeling like he was somehow in the wrong.

CHAPTER SEVEN

Henry's spirits rose a little as she finally saw the little town she called home through the open window of the stage. It had been a long slow process, but she was home after having spent a few nights sleeping in coach inns along the way, eating meals with her coach companions as they came and went, getting off at their destinations.

Walking home, she carried her saddlebags and waved at Jason as he ran to her, all smiles with King Richard the Lion Hearted at his side as usual.

"How's Richard been? That cut on his foot heal or do I need to work on it again?" she asked as she bent and patted the big red setter on his head, his long, feathered tail beating the air.

"Naw, he's all healed up, but I kept an eye on it like you taught me. No emergencies and no births so that's about it," Jason said walking to the house with her.

"I guess I'll have to move out again, but Doc, you think I can sleep in that room in the barn? I got it all cleaned out and put a cot frame in it. Just needs a mattress or some straw and it would be real comfy," the young boy said in a rush as if he'd been waiting to ask her this question for the couple of weeks she'd been away.

"If it's all right with your mom. I wouldn't mind, but you'd have to make do with my cooking," she teased because like most boys, Jason thought his mom was the best cook in the world.

"You don't cook so bad, Doc, just a little too fancy is all." He left to figure out a mattress for his new sleeping quarters.

Henry was able to rest a couple of days but was itching to get some kind of work. Sitting around gave her too much time to think about Tanner, and she wanted to put him out of her mind. Then out of her memory, which was going to take a lot longer.

The warm summer days soon brought the usual calls for a vet. A plow horse with a swollen leg, a hunting dog with large bumps that turned out to be larvae laid under its skin by blowflies, a sow with an impacted tooth. All things she could handle quickly and have the animal back to their owner and ready for work.

Jason came running to her with a request for her to go out to one of the area farms that had problems with their summer births. The cows were losing calves, going into labor much too soon. Henry saddled the horse she purchased since returning home and rode out to the farm hoping the cattle didn't have something contagious that could travel through the herds spread out over the acres of pasture lands they shared with other ranches.

The Texas longhorns seemed to bring a wasting disease wherever they went, and she feared this might be some sort of variation of that. If it were, there wasn't anything she could do to protect the local cattle. They would eventually bleed out and die in the pastures.

Luckily, it was only with the dairy herd so far.

Those animals were kept separate from the others except when they were freshening them to renew their milk supply. Then the bulls were brought into the paddocks and put with the cow to be covered. Henry checked over the three cows that lost their calves then asked to see the fields where they had grazed for the last few weeks.

The thin farmer was explaining, "We bring them up closer to the barn when they're getting near their time to keep an eye out for them, but this beats all. I'll lose one, maybe two if the weather's been bad, but to lose three so close together and for no reason. I mean you saw them, those calves were perfect, no reason to expel them early."

"No, and the cows are healthy and well nourished. I think we'll find the culprit out here, possibly along the fence line."

Henry began walking the fence staring at the ground and, every once in a while, kicked at a partially eaten plant. Then a quarter of a mile from the barn she stopped and squatted down fingering a green weed with the stems chewed down. She pulled it up, roots and all, pushing it into the seed bag she brought with her to collect samples.

"You've got Queen Ann's Lace growing here. The cows have already eaten the flowers off, but the rest of the plant is still here. This can cause the cows to go into early labor. It needs to be taken out of here, roots and all or the others will find it, too. I think it's terribly bitter, but animals will still eat it. No accounting for taste it seems." She pulled some of the still uneaten plants that were nearby.

"The worse culprit is this wooly loco. Hardly

recognizable, it's been eaten down so close to the ground. If one cow starts eating it for some reason the others will, too. You need to move these cows and then dig out those plant areas to clear the loco. It will depend on how much of the stuff each cow ate to determine whether she'll lose her calf or not."

"Geez, I never saw none of it. Must of eaten it as soon as it popped through. I thank ya, Doc. All right if I drop off a payment when I get to town?"

While the farmer and his sons walked the rest of the perimeter of the field, Henry rode home, her stomach a little queasy. Maybe she should have looked closer at those cows for illness and grinned at the idea of catching something from the bovine.

Jason came running up to take her horse as soon as Henry came into the back yard. Did the boy ever just walk? He could wear a body down simply watching him. Henry dismounted and held on to the saddle for a moment to steady herself. She felt a little dizzy, too. Maybe she was getting sick. Physician, heal thyself went through her mind, and she smiled at the irreverent thought.

"You all right, Doc? Can I get you anything? You look a little pale," Jason said all on top of each other. "I'll take Queen Rose and brush her down. Why don't you go on in and lay down for a while?" He led the mare into the stable.

"I may just do that. I haven't been sleeping very well. Must be the heat." Henry fabricated the reason for her tiredness. The real reason was lack of sleep. That when it was dark and she was lying in her bed, she wished Tanner was there with her, wished they could have had a calmer conversation about their needs and expectations.

But it had been weeks, and there hadn't been any signs of him, and now she needed to pull herself up by the bootstraps and continue with her life. It wasn't going to be the end of the world. She was older and wiser is all.

Waking from her nap feeling worse not better, Henry tried to drink some tea, but it didn't sit well. She soon was running for the sink to spill her gut into it, which thankfully wasn't much, only the few sips of tea she had gotten down. Wiping her mouth, she almost crawled back to the sofa which is where she was when the nausea hit her. It was getting dark and Jason came in to see why Henry hadn't lit the lamps or fed Richard.

"I can get his food if you want to just lay there, Doc," he offered.

"That would be good, Jason. I feel a little under the weather, but I'm sure I'll get better. Don't get too close to me, though. I don't want you taking this back to your family." She tried to lie as quiet as she could so as to not bring on another bout of vomiting.

"Do you want me to make you some tea or maybe soup?" he offered. "I've never seen you sick in the two years I've worked for you."

"No, thank you. I'll be fine with a little more rest. Just need to sleep through it." She was practically falling asleep as she spoke.

"I'll be right in the stable then if you need me. Should I leave Richard with you in case you need to send for me?" he asked, worried more than a little.

"No, really, Jason, I'm fine." She hoped she wasn't lying to the boy.

The next morning Henry woke up still on the sofa,

which was not a usual resting place for her. Sitting up, she felt back to normal. Cleaning up at her washstand and brushing her teeth, she changed into clean clothes feeling hungry for her missed meals. She called out to Jason to see what he wanted for breakfast as he brought in a basket of fresh eggs.

"Oh, those look good. I can fry up some and have some of the bread Mrs. Woods dropped off for taking care of her cat's ear," she said as she went about the kitchen heating water for tea for herself and pouring milk for Jason.

"I thought I could go to the livery and work with my brother today if that was all right with you," Jason said as he took off his hat, washed his hands, and sat at the table in his customary spot.

"Sure, that will be fine. If I need to go out on a call, I can saddle Rose. I'll see you this evening for dinner." She sat down after serving him several of the eggs.

Henry cut off a bite and popped it into her mouth then tried to chew. Instead, her eyes bugged out and she again found herself hunched over the sink heaving and then dry heaving. She never felt so sick in her life.

Jason sat quietly until Henry got herself under control. "My ma drank something that helped her when she was this way."

Henry couldn't help asking, "What way?"

"Expectin'," Jason answered and returned to eating his food as the one word penetrated Henry's consciousness.

"Don't tell anyone, please," was all she said before another wave of nausea tried to take over. Henry looked at Jason knowing the boy was right. Unable to fathom the problems she was going to need to face, including sending Jason back to his mother rather than allow him to be around an unmarried woman of evidently low morals.

"I think Ma could help you."

"It's not the same. Just don't say anything to anyone yet, please. I have things to work out," she said as she went and lay down on the sofa again, wanting the dizziness to go away, too. If every woman felt this badly when they were pregnant, Henry couldn't imagine going through it nine times as Jason's mother had.

Jason cleaned up the kitchen, filled the bucket with water, then left, telling her quietly he would be back later that day. Henry waved but didn't speak, trying to keep her mind off how badly she felt again. How badly she may feel for another two months.

Henry had learned about childbirth and the symptoms and problems associated with it during her medical training, but it was all coming home to her now.

Hypothetical illness was not the same as living through the symptoms. Perhaps knowledge isn't a good thing when you can gauge your physical feelings on a calendar, first three months of nausea, dizziness, fainting, light headedness followed by three months of tiredness, hunger, some swelling and discomfort, followed by three months of irritability, more swelling, hemorrhoids, and great discomfort finalizing in hours of painful labor and making a humiliating spectacle of yourself.

Presented like that, why hadn't Henry thought about this before she allowed herself to be so overwhelmed by lust and desire? She practically threw

Susan Payne

herself at Tanner. No wonder he had reservations about marrying her. Henry certainly hadn't presented herself as a woman a man would want to take home to his mother.

Thinking about undoing the past was too late. Henry needed to make plans for the future. She had pulled-up stakes before and started all over, and she could do it again. She hated to think of selling the little farm, but all her money was tied up in it, and she would need the money to begin again somewhere else.

Possibly try to pass herself off as a widow or that she was separated from her husband. She would need to think of something, and the first step always led back to leaving here and moving to where no one would look twice at a woman with a child.

One of the larger cities like Austin. No, not Austin, she might run into the Major or even Tanner there. God, she prayed, don't let her run into Tanner. Henry fell asleep on the sofa again. She heard Jason come in and whispered that he had taken care of Richard, then he left quietly saying his mother had been always tired, too.

Again, in the morning Henry felt quite well, but this time refrained from going into the kitchen or trying to cook or eat anything. She didn't want a repeat of yesterday. She hoped not eating would suffice in allowing her to move around during her usual daily activities.

Cleaning up in her bedroom, she changed clothes and still felt well so carefully decided she would try to wash some of the laundry, taking the large tub onto the back porch and boiling water.

Jason was cleaning the leather on the saddle when he glanced up to discover Tanner getting off his horse.

Tanner spoke first, "Jason, right? Want to take my horse and cool him off for me? He's had a long trip this morning and deserves a little care. And take Guinevere," he said referring to Henry's horse and saddle she sold in Melville.

"Sure, Ranger Tanner, I can do that. You come to make things right with the Doc?" he asked innocently.

"Make things, right? Yeah, I guess you can say that. Is she here?" he asked looking over to the house.

"Yeah, getting ready to do some wash," Jason said explaining the tub on the back stoop.

"Richard around?" Tanner asked, his voice hardening with the man's name.

Jason looked quizzically at Tanner, saying, "He's always around here somewhere. Never gets too far."

"Well, do me a favor and keep him busy out here. Don't let him go into the house until I finish talking with the Doc," Tanner said conspiratorially, just between men.

"Oh, Richard isn't allowed into the house. Not since he broke the Doc's teapot," Jason explained.

Tanner knew Jason wasn't allowed in the house when Henry was there and was kind of glad to hear Richard wasn't allowed in either. Knowing the other man evidently didn't stay the nights made Tanner's hopes rise. Maybe he had a chance to change Henry's mind about giving them a chance to spend time together.

Pushing his hat back on his head, Tanner strode into the house without knocking, wanting to catch Henry off guard, before she could set up any barricades between them. He wanted a frank discussion, and he wanted to leave this farm with Henry right beside him.

He found her sorting a few pieces of clothes in the bedroom as he filled the doorway and announced, "We have to talk, Henry."

He held each side of the door trying to keep his hands from reaching out to her as he wanted. All he ended up doing was startling Henry so much the blood rushed from her head and she put out her hands to make sure she would land on the bed.

Tanner realized what happened and went to her, kneeling, taking her small hands in his, apologizing for the macho stunt. "I'm sorry Darlin'. I didn't mean to surprise you that much, but I was so glad to see you, I came on a little too strong. Let me help you stand."

Henry, unable to speak in case she threw up all over his well-cared for boots, shook her head and remained sitting, trying not to move too much. Finally, feeling able to speak she began, "You did startle me. What brings you back here?"

Tanner looked at her, his brows together in worry or anger. "You did, Doc. I've wanted to talk with you, but the Major sent me first to Abilene then to Laredo. Finally, I told him I would send in my resignation if he didn't give me the time off I'd been asking for to come and see you."

Being able to hold onto her stomach contents seemed to be diminishing by the moment. Henry simply wanted Tanner out of her house and away from her before he guessed what was wrong with her. "We spoke right before I left, and I think we were both quite clear."

"I wasn't clear. I wasn't clear with anything. I

thought we were leaving town together, as a couple. I didn't expect to find you had sold up everything and left me. Then the Major wouldn't let me change assignments, insisted I go to Abilene, and that took a couple of weeks."

He seemed frustrated, but the more he talked the less she needed to.

"Marshal Clinton was facing a mess after the shooting at Pine Street in January. The city put in a lot of new laws that aren't popular with the drifters hanging around the bars and such.

"A deputy and his brother, a city councilman, were shot and killed. Now a new marshal's been put in place, and I was backup till he could hire his own deputy. Then the Major kept putting me in another town, another job, keeping me away from you. But not anymore, we need to talk. I'll take on Richard if I have to, but the two of us belong together. I'll tell him that just before I send his teeth down his throat," he told her adamantly.

Henry looked up at him with watery, worried eyes then ran into the kitchen, just making the sink once more. Could anything be worse?

Following, Tanner found her clutching the edges of the sink as he pulled a chair over for her to rest on.

"You're sick," he stated. "Why didn't you say so? This can wait a while now I'm here. I have a few days before the Major's going to order me anywhere."

"I don't want you to stay," she got out without adding another bout of heaving to her humiliation.

"I won't leave you, not again. I should have followed you that day and to hell with the Major and his plans. You're more important to me than anything else." Tanner sounded sincere.

"I don't want you here. I can take care of us, myself." Henry wondered if she gave herself away but felt calmer when Tanner didn't seem to think anything about what she said.

"And I told you I was here to stay, at least long enough for me to convince you we belong together." He glanced around the kitchen asking, "How can I help you? You look like something the cat dragged in, if you don't mind me telling you."

Pale and drawn, Henry peered up at him saying, "I should have thrown up on your boots." Then proceeded to do so to both their surprise.

Henry woke to find herself tucked up in her bed, the shades drawn, and the sound of crockery rattling in the kitchen. She closed her eyes when she heard footsteps approaching the door.

"I know you're awake, I can see your eyes moving beneath the lids. Here, try some of this, it may help. I remember my mother with my siblings eating these things like they were candy. Come on, try them."

At the promise of some relief from the nausea, Henry opened her eyes to see a much-refreshed Tanner who must have washed-up after his ride here. Clean shaven and smiling, something he hadn't done before her throwing up on him.

"Sorry about your boots, I really didn't mean to do that. It simply hits me all of a sudden, and it's either run and throw up or evidently sit there and throw up. I don't know how women have more than one," she told him honestly.

"It must get better, and I think most of them think

it worth it in the end. Or they forget about all of it until it happens all over again," he teased helping her sit up and hang her feet over the edge. She noticed there was a pan sitting next to her bed, conveniently placed.

"You don't have to eat anything, but you might want to try just some dry toast or these soda crackers. My mother also swore on ginger root, so I went and bought some and made a little tea of it. Take it slow and see what works. You can't keep being sick or you'll dehydrate yourself," he informed her unnecessarily, since Henry was well aware of the dangers to her body without fluids.

She took the mug with shaking fingers and held it up to her nose. Her stomach didn't roll in protest, so she tried a little sip. The warm liquid ran down her throat and for once, stayed. She felt as if she had accomplished something of great importance.

"So, you figured it out? Too bad you weren't quicker and you could have saved your boots." She'd noticed he was only wearing socks.

"They've seen worse. I left them outside the back door when I got back from the store." At her worried expression, he said, "Don't worry, I cleaned them off before showing up at the gossip mill you call a general store. I had to answer some very cryptic questions, but I think I kept your reputation intact." Then took the mug from her shaking hands.

"They'll figure it out sooner or later. I was planning on moving to a larger city, possibly say I was a widow or something," she told him, lying back down although she felt more vulnerable to him in that position.

"So, you're planning on keeping it? The baby, I

mean?" he asked quietly, seeming to know he was on rocky ground. "I found some Queen Ann's Lace in the stable in a bag, I thought maybe…" Then he finished harshly, "I thought you hated me enough to get rid of my child, our child."

"No!" she answered adamantly. "I cleared the plant out of a farmer's field. As for the other, I was trying to find a way for this child to grow up in a world that won't punish it for the sins of its mother." Unwanted tears filled her eyes and ran onto the pillow slip.

Tanner went to the edge of the bed and sat down, lifting an unresisting Henry. "Hush, Darlin', there wasn't any sinning going on. We just anticipated our wedding vows a little. It happens every day I'm sure, nothing that a few words from a holy man won't fix."

"But you don't want to marry me, you said so. I wasn't good enough." Then the tears began to flow in earnest, and she couldn't control them.

She cried for the nights of loneliness she felt since leaving him, cried for her loss of trusting herself, cried for losing the only man she'd ever love. There could be no marriage between them. She certainly wouldn't force Tanner into changing his life to meet the needs of a wife and family.

He placed his hand on her shaking back and let her cry it out.

"I never said that. I never thought that at all. I was afraid of the strong feelings I had for you, that I felt you had for me. I felt I wasn't good enough for you. You're beautiful and educated and talented and smart. I'm just a cowboy with a gun and badge. That's all I'll ever be," he told her truthfully.

"I remember the expression on your face in the

room that morning, and it wasn't of a man who wanted to be married, no matter if I was already carrying your child. But don't beat yourself up over this. It happens, and I already feel more positive about my future. I'll figure things out. Thank you for coming and talking with me. I think everything will be all right for me from now on." She pushed him away and sat on the edge of the bed again to see if she could eat a cracker or two, get better so he would feel he could leave her again.

"I was finishing cleaning up the kitchen after feeding Jason. I'm going to sleep in the other room, but if you need me just call. I can be here in a minute," he told her looking at her in concern as she nodded sadly. "We'll talk then when you're up to it."

Again, the next morning, Henry felt fine and hurriedly cleaned herself keeping an eye on the door and berating herself for never installing locks. After brushing her teeth, she donned a simple dress that she swore felt tighter already. But that couldn't be possible, could it? She never missed having a mother until now, and the wave of sadness washing over her almost had her sobbing again.

"I'm heating more water for tea. Do you feel like trying anything more?" Tanner asked from outside the closed door.

"No, I ate a couple of crackers and so far, so good, but I don't want to push my luck," she called back picking up yesterday's tray to take out to the kitchen.

Tanner was pleased to see Henry looking more like her old self. She seemed rested and not so low, so sad, as she had the day before.

"The water's about ready," he said to break the ice between them.

He couldn't believe it took him more than a minute yesterday to realize she was running from him and another minute to realize he should chase after her. He never had to chase a woman to have her listen to him before, but Henry was full of surprises it seemed. It proved he would have to approach this a different way than what he first planned.

"Has Rich... I mean has the dog been fed?" she asked almost slipping with the name.

"Jason already told me Richard was the dog's name, when he told me his swishing tail was the reason he wasn't allowed in the house. Why'd you let me think it was another man? A man you were interested in?" he asked setting the cup of tea in front of her.

"Why do you think? You had basically told me I wasn't the kind of woman a man marries, and I let you think there was someone who wanted to marry me. So, now you know you were right and no one wants me. Can you hand me the sugar?" she said bluntly.

"That's not what I said and it's not true. Why do you insist on saying things like that? That degrade you and what we have together?" Tanner said almost slamming the sugar jar down on the table in anger.

"I'm sorry if I misread you. It still boiled down to the fact I was good enough to bed, but not good enough to wed. I must have a pillow cross-stitched with that to help me remember why I need to sleep alone," she said, losing all interest in the tea. "Sorry, I guess I shouldn't have gotten out of bed, I'm not fit company. Just leave the dishes, I'll do them after you're gone." Getting up, she began walking to her room.

"Rest if you need to, but I'll still be here when you wake up. I told you I wasn't leaving you again, and I meant it." He remained seated at the table with a cup of coffee in front of him.

Henry went to her room, and just to be obstinate, her body refused to be tired after the past few days of wanting to sleep every minute. She lay there staring up at the ceiling, wishing she would hear Tanner's horse leaving with him on it. Now she was a prisoner in her own home, just when she was feeling good enough to do something besides clasp a pan to her face.

Although Henry knew worry wasn't good for her, wasn't good for anyone, she couldn't prevent herself from thinking of the future and how she would provide for her child. She thought seriously of going back into medical practice, possibly with an established doctor. But not family practice, someone specializing in another field like tuberculosis or even the infirm. A hospital doctor with set hours and limited patient contact. That might work for her, and she could hire a nurse and later a nanny to care for the child.

For the first time, Henry could smile about the thought of the child, a small bundle like she had seen the mothers holding in the birthing wards where she trained. Then the little children running in the park and it seemed just like Jason, they were always in a hurry while calling out for their mothers to see this or look at that.

Henry felt more optimistic now. Nothing had changed really. It simply didn't seem so overwhelming any longer. She felt stronger and knew she could handle whatever she needed to. She drifted off and slept without the usual nightmares and anxious dreams that had been plaguing her recently.

Tanner sat in the chair, leaning back on the two rear legs, balancing there, watching Henry sleep, her eyes unmoving and her body relaxed and quiet. He smiled as he thought about being able to see her like this any time he wanted. Having the right to sit with her, watch over her, protect her from all sorts of evils and bad things.

But then the worries infringed on his thinking. What if he couldn't protect her from the evils? He was on assignment so often, and she and their child would be left alone. Who would protect them then? And Tanner knew there were all sorts of evils and people out there that want to do nothing more than harm the innocent and pure.

To him, Henry was both of those. Her inner good, her wanting to help was what caused them to meet and work together in the first place. She endangered herself trying to protect women she didn't know and would never know. Now she had the baby to protect, too.

How were they to make a family, though, if she wouldn't believe in his feelings for her? How could he prove to her he had returned to marry her and that was before knowing she was carrying his child? Hell, he had so much feeling for her he'd marry her if she said she was carrying another man's child. And he would love it as much as he already did his own.

He should have followed her when she left Melville and none of this would be happening. Now he would need to remind her of everything they had felt for one another in that hotel room. But how do you make love with a woman who can't stop heaving her cookies?

Henry rolled over to see it was dark outside her

shaded window and caught a movement out of the corner of her eye. Tanner was in her small chair she used to sit in when she did her hair, not really big enough for a man, let alone a man Tanner's size.

"You'll get a crick in your neck trying to sleep in that chair," she warned him.

"Too late, I already have a crick in my neck. How are you feeling now?" he asked sitting forward and peering into the darkness at her.

"I think I'm pretty good. I think I'm actually hungry," she said in surprise.

"Do you want some chicken? I roasted one, and I can warm it up." At her silence, he assured her, "Jason said it was all right to eat them. That you don't name them so they're not really pets."

"No, they're not pets. We simply refer to them as Chickens of the Round Table and they have their place in the food chain. I just wasn't sure if I should eat solids yet," she answered honestly, testing the thought of chicken in her mind's stomach. "I'll try some, but I'll have it cold. I don't want much. I think I need to get back to eating something besides tea again."

"Do you need help getting up?" he asked solicitously.

"I'm not feeble, Tanner, and this malaise will go away."

"When?" he asked trying not to sound too anxious, but he felt he had to keep his hands to himself while she was ill, and he did his best convincing with his hands.

"In about six weeks, more or less," she said as she preceded him out the door into the parlor then to the kitchen.

Tanner's heart dropped like a rock, thinking of

Susan Payne

ways to keep himself from rushing her but, damn, six weeks more or less? That was a hell of a long time for him to stay away from the woman he loved and remain in the same house with her. He said he wasn't going to leave without her, and he meant it.

He'd wire the Major and let him know he needed a break, or he could accept the wire as his resignation. Tanner was more intent on getting Henry to marry him than ever. If she wouldn't listen to sense, he'd sit on her front step until the baby was born so everyone would know the father hadn't abandoned his family.

Cutting off a chicken leg, Henry sat at the table gingerly taking little bites off it, letting it settle before taking another bite. She glanced at Tanner watching intently. "I'm fine, Tanner, now please don't hover. I think the worse is over or it's taking a break or something's going on. I feel almost normal. Stop watching me like a pot ready to boil over." Smiling, she let him know she was feeling better. "Of course, you do have reason to look at me expecting something to happen after our last visit to this room."

"The water's hot. Do you want some tea?" he asked trying not to crowd her.

"Some of my own please. Let's see if I'm really better."

"I'm not wearing my boots so it's all right if you miss the sink, although last time it had to have been planned. I mean that sink is a lot bigger than my boots, yet you missed it completely." He enjoyed seeing her smile as she raised her eyebrows at him looking smug.

That evening she read some of the book by Jules Verne aloud to him. Tanner had his eyes closed, but he wasn't sleeping. "I wonder if this Verne character really

114

knows what he's writing about. Do you think any of those things will one day be real? Boats underwater and that sort of thing?"

"Anything can happen, I think. There are the ironclads, it was a submerged, and the use of hot-air balloons for travel is being attempted all over Europe. I mean look at the changes in guns in the past couple of decades. We could have gotten rid of the British a lot faster if the colonists had a Gatling gun, I'm sure." Henry let the book lie open over her body.

"Or ice-making machines. Now we can get fresh strawberries clear across the continent and shrimp and meats. It wasn't so long ago no one even heard of a pineapple let alone ate one. Steam engines will soon run all kinds of things besides farm equipment and trains. I understand there's a sewing machine that can stitch heavy sail cloth like a hot knife through butter."

Tanner had been sitting beside her, and he couldn't help himself as he reached over and laid his hand intimately over her stomach.

Henry jumped at his touch then softened knowing he was trying to be open with her. "Tanner, this child will be your child. I'll let you know where I settle, but my having this baby isn't a reason to change your whole life. You can continue as you always have been. I'll be fine," she said gently, letting him know there were no recriminations or blame to be had. She was ready to continue making plans, the baby would arrive and she would be its mother.

"I can't believe it's really in there. I mean I don't doubt it and I've seen other women get large and then there's a baby, but this, this is something I had a part of, we both had a part in making it. I don't know if I'll ever get over the amazing way creation works," he told her, his hand still on her body.

"And I can handle it alone. I know seeing me the last couple of days makes you doubt that. All women have some form of morning sickness, and I'll live through it, miserable as it seems. You can go back and do what you were going to do before we met."

"I don't want to leave without you."

"I think you're a good man, a kind man, and an honorable man, but you never expected to marry me. I was a distraction on your assignment, and I went into this with my eyes wide-open. I don't regret what we did. I'll look back on it in my old age and smile, but it will be a small part of my life by then. One night of many years of nights. Please feel free to go, to leave me be. I have come to realize this is part of my fate, and I don't think you were ever meant to be a part of my life." She sadly met his gaze. Even if it hurt to say these things to him, even if it hurt him a little—the truth often did.

Tanner needed to confess. "I wanted you with me after you left. I felt lost and unhappy and as if I was missing something, a piece of me missing. I went to Abilene as ordered and couldn't keep my mind on the job. I kept wanting to come back to the tent and tell you what I'd done that day. Share my day, I guess. I don't want to pressure you, not now, not in your condition, but I'm not walking away, either. I came to convince you we should be together. I'll wait right here in this town if you don't want me here in the house. I'll wait until you realize you need me, too."

"I think you'll get bored. You're a Ranger, and eventually that will win out. You can stay for as long as

I'm here, but that may not be much longer. I want to leave by the time I start to show I'm with child. What the people in town are thinking about my house guest, I can hardly wait to hear. If anyone is brave enough to tell me." She placed the bookmark on the page she finished reading and laid it on the table next to the sofa.

"I'll prove myself to you. I'll be here until you finally realize I'm right, that we belong together," he said as he watched her go to her room.

CHAPTER EIGHT

The next day Jason came running toward Tanner as he brushed down his horse, figuring he would take him out for some exercise and get to know the town a little better.

"Ranger Tanner, Ranger Tanner, I have a wire for you." He waved the piece of paper in the air.

Tanner swore under his breath damning the Major if he had sent orders already knowing things weren't going as well with Henry as he had hoped. Henry came out the back door at Jason's yelling walking forward wiping her hands on a kitchen towel.

Grabbing the message, he opened it roughly, expecting to see the Major's name at the bottom. It was, but the message was completely unexpected. Tanner's hands trembled.

Henry asked worriedly, "What is it, Tanner? Something wrong with the Major?"

"No, it's from the Major informing me my parents are dead," he said, his voice void of emotion.

"Oh, Tanner, I'm so sorry. What about your brother and sister, are they all right?" she asked.

He looked at the short message as most wires were. "They must be all right. It doesn't include them. It was a train accident it seems, and their train car fell off the tracks and tipped down an embankment. I can't believe it. My mother would have loved you, Henry, she wanted another daughter she said to make the number of females equal in the family. We voted on things and she got tired of losing." Tanner still hadn't shown much emotion other than the trembling.

"I'm sorry I didn't get to meet her, Tanner. I know you thought highly of her, which means she was pretty special. Can I get you some food and supplies for the trip home? You'll want to leave as soon as possible, I'm sure."

Tanner wadded the message in his large hand. "I'm not leaving you. I told you that already." The fierceness in his voice made Jason step back and look at Henry with big sad eyes.

"Jason, could you finish with the horses and I'll get back with you about packing. Tanner and I need some private time to discuss how to go on." She walked into the house knowing Tanner would follow her.

He seemed to be in shock but didn't say anything more as she sat him in a kitchen chair and dug back into her pantry to bring out a bottle of whiskey. Pouring a good amount into a glass, she handed it to Tanner, telling him, "Drink this, then we'll talk."

Glancing up at her, he nodded, downing the golden liquid in one mouthful without coughing or choking. "I'm fine, it was just a shock. I was planning on visiting them soon, hopefully bringing you with me. Like I said, she would have loved you—and her grandchild, of course."

Henry began to tear up and said again, "I'm so sorry Tanner, but you mustn't stay here with me. Your brother and sister will need you. They're so young neither will know how to go on. Please think what your parents would expect you to do."

"I can't leave without you. I'll lose you, and you and the baby need me, too. You just don't know it yet." He spoke without emotion although he saw the tears rolling down her cheeks and put out his hand to catch them.

"Oh, Tanner, don't make this about me. Please go and take care of your family. They need you more than I do." She must have realized how that sounded to him and added, "I mean they need you more right now."

Shaking his head, he told her, "I'll send a wire telling my father's attorney what to do, and we have a ranch foreman who can take over the ranch's daily work. Sounds like maybe he was already doing so since my parents were both on the train. They must have been taking a trip. They had been doing that lately."

"You can't handle this kind of loss over the telegraph wire. Please wait to make any kind of decision until the shock wears off. I'll get you another drink, you're much too pale yet," she told him, but he didn't answer her, simply stared at the wadded ball of paper in his hand.

After half an hour, Tanner began to move normally again asking for paper, pen, and ink, which Henry got from her desk drawer. Handing them to him, she noticed he was making a list of things he wanted the attorney to do and how his parents should be dressed for the coffins. Oh, my God, he was making the arrangements from here, even planning on missing the funeral when his siblings would need him the most.

"Tanner, you can't do it like this. Those children need you now." As he began to shake his head and say something, Henry put her finger over his lips. "I'll go with you. I have months to get myself settled. This cannot wait. I'll pack, and you decide whether we should take the horses and go to the closest town with a train or whether to take a coach and leave the horses here."

Tanner looked at her asking, "You're not just saying this to get me to go are you, Henry? You wouldn't be that unkind, would you?"

"No, I am not that unkind, Tanner. Let's get moving because if we are to leave by coach we'll need to be out of here in a couple of hours. Send Jason to let them know we want two tickets if we're not riding." She headed to the bedroom thinking what she needed to take with her.

Worriedly, Tanner followed her. "Henry, this coach trip isn't harmful for you, is it? For the baby? I won't jeopardize either of you."

"No, I can take a little trip anywhere. The baby and I are quite safe. I wouldn't go otherwise. Come help me get this trunk open then send for the tickets since it seems we'll be going by coach. I can take all I'll need for a couple of weeks this way. Do you want Jason's brother to take your horse to the train and put him on it?" she asked trying to keep Tanner focused and keep him from taking advantage and asking her to make promises she wasn't able to give at this time.

"No, I'll come back here for him. I won't let you travel alone again. Once was more than enough." He left her packing, saying, "I'll go tell Jason to let the coach company know there will be two more passengers for the stage this afternoon."

Both Tanner and Henry were dressed and waiting as the horses were exchanged and the mail bag put up into the driver's seat. The Shotgun got onto the seat next to the driver, and they left after less than half an hour stop-over. As it happened, Tanner and Henry were the only passengers. As the coach swayed out of town on the dirt road, Tanner scooped Henry onto his lap and pushed her head onto his shoulder.

"Try to rest, and I'll see if I can limit the amount of jostling you have to go through. When we get to the train it will be a much smoother ride, especially compared to this," he said with a smile, trying to make her feel better.

Henry stayed in his arms because it did feel less bumpy. At least she wasn't being hit into the sides of the coach, and he was warm and rather comfortable to rest against.

"If your arm goes numb it's your own fault," she said as she let him hold her. This was the closest they'd been since she conceived her child, no, since she conceived *their* child. Henry would have to admit there were two parents now. She would need to make plans that would include Tanner in some way. She knew she could never cut him out completely now.

Henry slept and woke a couple of times to find Tanner bracing his boot against the opposite seat to keep them from sliding off their bench. The coach ride hadn't gotten any smoother, but Henry insisted on getting onto the seat and giving Tanner's legs a rest. At the next stop, another passenger joined them, a salesman travelling to the following town where he would disembark and remain.

Feeling a little nauseous, Henry was hoping it didn't show. She didn't want Tanner to quit this trip part way through because she was sick again. They couldn't stop living for the next two months, so she would have to function around this pregnancy—and she could.

Two salesmen joined the last leg of their journey, both loquacious and eager to brag to one another about the number and size of their accounts. Henry remained quietly by Tanner's side as he tried to buffer the more severe of the jolts that reverberated inside the coach. The two other men accepted the collisions into one another as the normal part of travelling by this method of conveyance and struck up a conversation.

Tanner had gotten fidgety, which was unlike him. Was he afraid they were going to miss their train and need to wait another day? She didn't think the coach was running late, the two salesmen didn't seem to worry about the time.

Glancing at his pocket watch again, Tanner finally whispered into her ear, "I think I cut this a little too close. I didn't want to upset you on the trip with any more surprises, but I think we need to talk privately. We won't have more than a necessary stop before we get to the town where we'll catch our train."

"So, you're not afraid we'll miss the connection? The way you kept checking your watch, I thought possibly we hadn't enough time. I could have stayed with the bags and gotten the next train out so you could get to your family sooner." She offered to give him another option if he hadn't thought of her doing that.

"I'm not leaving you." He was whispering and glancing toward the two other men to make sure they weren't paying attention to his words. "That's the issue. I can't bring an unmarried woman home with me to present to my younger brother and sister. And someone might guess your condition, then all hell will break loose with the neighbors. They all think they have a say in my life, it's like having a beehive of nosy aunts," he groused.

Quietly she tried to sooth him. "That should be comforting because if they take that kind of interest in you then they'll also care for Jessie and Jenna. But you mustn't take longer than absolutely necessary. I can make my own way, I promise," she assured him, but she could tell he wasn't convinced.

"Just promise you won't run from me, hide back home when I'm least expecting it. I don't know what I'd do if you left me now."

"I told you, already. I will go to your family and stay there until the children are in capable hands or able to live on their own. It sounds more and more as if they will have plenty of people caring for them. You can return to the Rangers, and I'll return home to make my plans." She reassured him in a reasonable tone yet too quietly for the salesmen to hear as they continued their discussion on the benefits of the steam engine in manufacturing.

Tanner became quiet again but hadn't relaxed. Henry could feel his tenseness as they continued on the stage. The other men checked their watches and smiled saying they were almost into town and the rigors of the trip would be forgotten over a drink and steak dinner. It seemed the two strangers were now bosom buddies and would continue their debate long into the night. Henry couldn't deny she would love to stand on *terra firma* again.

What must it be like to cross the ocean to Europe? That trip takes more than a month and a half, and the rolling waves would be a nightmare. At least with the stage she was able to get out every few hours as horses were changed or sleep in an inn if the trip were longer. As it was, she would spend the night sitting upright on the train since they wired for their tickets so late there weren't any sleeping berths available.

As the stage pulled into town across from the train station, they finally left the confines of their less than comfortable ride. Tanner turned to Henry and said seriously, "Do you trust me?"

Concerned, Henry answered truthfully, "Yes, of course."

In a rush, he continued, "I wired a friend to arrange for a minister to meet us here and perform a wedding ceremony before the train left. That way you and I don't have to lie to anyone or hide what we mean to one another. The baby will have my name, and when you leave, if you leave, then you won't need to lie about being a widow with some poor dead husband.

"You can say we separated because my job as a Ranger was too stressful or we didn't suit or whatever you want to say. I'll go along with it, I promise. But I couldn't think of a way to bring you home, keep you beside me without this permanent arrangement between us."

He gazed into her eyes hopefully, whispering, "Don't scream at me or worse, stomp off into the crowded streets. It would take forever to find you."

Lowering her gaze, she shook her head in despair. "Oh, Tanner, how could you do such a thing and not mention it?" That was all Henry could think to say to the distraught man in front of her.

"I tried, but you were tired, and I thought you

would be more open to it if you were well rested. Then we got company in the coach, and then it was too late. We're here, and I see my friend waving, and I want to protect you so badly." He was pleading for forgiveness.

"I'll do it," she said bluntly. "Just promise me no more surprises or I swear I will find a way to get back home even if I have to walk."

A smile broke across Tanner's face as he promised, "I'll make sure it never comes to that."

Turning, he put out his hand to meet his approaching friend. "Emory, this is my soon to be wife, Henrietta. I assume by your grin you've been able to contact a minister for us?"

"Good to meet the woman who is going to civilize this guy. We've spent quite a bit of time on the trails together until he took that cushy position in Austin. Gets all the soft jobs now. No more running across the border after bushwhackers," Emory teased, slapping his friend on the back.

"Is the ceremony going to be close or do we need a buggy?" asked Tanner, seeming too nervous to talk with the friend he hadn't seen in several months.

"I've never seen a bridegroom so anxious, but then I can see why with such a beautiful fiancée. In answer to your question, we can walk to the church. You can see the tall spire from here," he said, grinning in amusement at Tanner's demise as a bachelor.

Taking Henry's arm, Tanner slowed his pace to her shorter stride. He soon relaxed enough to question Emory about his life and family, more consistent with two friends meeting after a time apart. Henry, too, became calmer as they approached the double doors leading into the Methodist church.

Once inside, Emory leaned over saying, "I took the privilege of getting you some flowers and a family Bible to begin your life together. I knew it would take a special woman to hogtie this maverick, and I don't think I was wrong. Do you want me to walk you down the aisle? I have an organist. Actually, she's the minister's wife, who is also the second witness and couldn't be dissuaded. She insists all brides wish to approach their groom to the sound of a triumphant march."

Henry smiled, the rest of any concern leaving her mind and body as she took Emory's arm that he held out toward her. Realizing Tanner was only trying to protect her and their child, she needed to think the same way. Protect her child from ridicule, from curious eyes, from a society that had dirty little names for what her child was without a father's last name.

The organ's bellows wheezed with their intake of air, and a resounding rendition of a march more often heard at military parades than weddings began. Henry and Emory grinned at each other conspiratorially as they began the long trip down the aisle. Tanner was waiting with a grim expression as if he were facing the gallows. Henry had the greatest urge to laugh, but only the smile escaped.

Tanner responded to that smile, letting his wide-open grin shine out, seeming to relax now he realized she wasn't going to run at any moment or turn him down flat when the important question was asked by the minister.

Emory handed Henry into Tanner's care then took his place next to him. The reverend began the ceremony Henry could have told him by heart after going to so many of her friends' weddings. When it came to the ring part, Tanner surprised her again when he handed the minister the wedding band to bless then placed a keeper ring onto her finger afterward.

Tanner bestowed a tender kiss when instructed to by the minister, and Emory was allowed a small peck on her cheek as well. The two men shook hands at the door of the church and Tanner, in a much lighter mood, walked Henry back toward the train station.

"Do you want anything to eat, some tea maybe? I noticed you haven't eaten anything, and that worries me," he told her, trying not to nag at her, but he was concerned.

"I thought it best this way. Don't worry, I'll make up for it later, and then you'll be worrying about how fat I'm getting."

He stopped in the middle of the sidewalk saying earnestly, "Never. You'll always be perfect to me no matter what you do to change."

"Oh, Tanner, you say that now, but I'm going to get old and wrinkled and cranky," she told him seriously.

"And so am I. Do you expect me to stay as I am? Living marks a man. Hopefully, I'll still be able to make love to my wife."

He smiled, then the smile slipped as he realized what he had said. "But I don't expect to. Make love with you, that is. The ceremony will make sure you and the baby are taken care of if anything happens to me and I can't be there for you. I'm not expecting anything to happen between us. Please don't worry I'll try to take advantage of this situation…" At her deep inhaling of breath as if to argue, he continued, "Take advantage of this situation again. I'll let you decide everything from now on."

Henry turned away and began walking toward the train while Tanner stayed a foot behind her knowing he might have pushed the boundaries too far already.

There was a short wait before the train pulled into the station and a few more minutes before the passengers disembarked and the freight and luggage exchanged.

They sat quietly while Henry fingered the rings on her now gloved hand. Tanner was keeping his distance knowing she wasn't in any mood for him to toy with her, but he was happier and calmer than he had been during the last half of their coach trip.

Henry was becoming sleepy again, he could tell, but at least the nausea she suffered wasn't going to go volatile all over the other passengers as she sat next to the window. He hoped watching the passing views would take her mind off the never-ending sickness.

Tanner was being very careful not to touch Henry or be too solicitous. It evidently made her cranky, feeling less than competent and independent. He knew there were still a lot of miles between them and the ranch. He wished he'd thought to bring her a pillow or something to buffer her from the jostling of the train. It would be considerably less than the stage, but still a lot of swaying and clanking, and it had been a long day already.

After a night of trying to sleep on the train, Tanner could foresee Henry being too tired to continue to the ranch. He would cross that bridge when they came to it. Right now, he was trying to make her comfortable without appearing to be too solicitous.

While the train was still quiet, Tanner encouraged Henry to close her eyes and sleep, hoping she would be tired enough to stay sleeping through most of the evening and following night. He would forego supper, too, and watch over her.

A little girl with a basket came through selling muffins and fresh peaches.

"Oh, the peaches sound lovely," Henry said.

Tanner called the young girl over, her pigtails neatly tied with yarn matching her frock. She wasn't very old, and he thought her sweet.

"I'll take a couple of the peaches and two muffins," Tanner told the child, and she gave them to him wrapped in a piece of cloth. Tanner gave her fifty cents and the girl went to make change and he told her to keep it. She thanked him then moved farther down the car as another passenger called to her.

"That was nice of you, Tanner. I don't know why you insist on thinking of yourself as unworthy." She snuggled against him as he found no answer to her words.

Henry spent most of the evening leaning against Tanner's shoulder, only being displaced when he had to use the necessary, which she took advantage of, too. Another benefit of traveling on a train rather than a coach. No wonder this mode of travel was so popular.

They both dozed off and on throughout the night and woke as other passengers began moving about in the early morning. There was a line forming for the necessary, and they waited their turn patiently.

The train was due into Summerville before lunch. The town closest to the Tanner ranch in an area where they measured acres per cow rather than cows per acre.

Water, especially in the summer, was scarce, but Tanner explained the ranch had a good well supply with windmills keeping the galvanized tubs full. Henry listened knowing he needed to talk to keep his mind off what was ahead of them. She knew Tanner had difficult times in front of him.

Henry was barely able to make out shadows in the pre-dawn sky. Huge barns indicated large numbers of livestock and winter stores of hay. There were also fields ready for harvest, rice or some other grain, possibly feed grain. It was too dark to tell at this distance.

She began seeing a few lights in the windows as they passed the smaller towns that didn't earn a stop on this train's schedule. She let her eyes drift down and before she realized it, Tanner was nudging her gently saying she might want to refresh herself before they needed to debark. Daylight was coming in all the windows up and down the car.

In the necessary, she checked her hair and hat, which both needed straightening. Wiping her face with a wet handkerchief, she thought she appeared to have been dragged through a hedge backward then run over. Whatever would Tanner's siblings think of her? Well, she would soon find out as Tanner informed her, they would get to the ranch after about an hour ride.

CHAPTER NINE

The whistle announced its arrival in the morning air as the train began slowing down. Henry should force Tanner to get a meal before trying to drive them out to the ranch. Maybe if she told him she was hungry he would eat, too.

Pulling down their one small satchel and his hat from the upper shelf over their heads, Tanner stood back so Henry could proceed him out of the train. Once on the platform, Henry stood near the building to wait or their luggage, and Tanner disappeared to locate it and figure out where to rent the buggy.

There was a scurry of happy squeals, and Tanner was holding a very pretty, young woman, her arms clutched around his neck as she happily cried out, "Oh, Daniel, you got here. You got here. I'm so glad you made it in time."

Tanner put the young woman, wearing a pretty gingham dress with ruffles around the hem touching the ground, so this was no schoolroom miss, from his body. This must be his sister, Jenna. Henry watched as Tanner's gaze searched the platform until he spotted an even younger boy and called him over.

He lowered his arms he had held out for a hug when the young man approached with his hand out to shake his older brother's. Tanner met Jessie on the boy's terms and shook hands with him like a man.

Then Jessie, wearing trousers, white shirt with vest, and well cared for boots of a working rancher folded his arms across his chest, not knowing what else to do with his limbs.

Jenna was again clinging to Tanner's arm as Jessie began to get a mulish expression on his face.

Henry had been concerned about this very thing. Tanner only stopped back home occasionally, mostly around holidays. Now Jessie, who had been his dad's right-hand man, was worried Tanner was coming home and possibly taking over the ranch, completely putting Jessie out in the cold. The boy was only sixteen but had spent all sixteen years on that ranch. Seeing his older sister hang on Tanner wasn't helping his disposition any either, Henry could tell.

Tanner listened to Jenna and folded the young woman into his arms again. Jessie appeared as if he was about to cry, also. They must have been discussing their parents, perhaps how to go about getting the funeral arranged.

Henry remained where she was, knowing it was important the siblings reconnect without another distraction interfering. She would be introduced after the family had formed its bonds again. There was plenty of time to add another person when they drove home.

Finally, Tanner seemed to remember himself and turned to find Henry standing on the now almost deserted platform as the train pulled out of the station continuing its way to California.

"Oh, come meet your new sister-in-law. I didn't have time to even write home yet, but Henry, I mean

Henrietta, will be staying with us until things get straightened out with the lawyers and everything," he said, turning hopefully toward Henry for agreement.

"I'm so sorry for your loss. I was looking forward to meeting your parents. This couldn't have been at a worse time for you, so sudden." Henry acknowledged each with a kiss on their cheek, having to go up on her tiptoes to reach Jessie. He was going to be as tall as Tanner when he was full grown.

"How did you know we would be on this train?" Henry asked knowing they hadn't been sure if they could catch the train the day before. Turning to Tanner, she asked, "Did you get time to send a wire?"

The two younger Tanners became quiet staring at the platform. "Our parents are coming on the next train," Jenna said trying to keep the tears from sliding down her cheek. "The burial is scheduled for tomorrow morning at the ranch's cemetery. The minister is coming from our church to say a few words."

Taking a deep breath, Henry said, "Then I'm glad we made it in time to be with you."

A whistle sounded as the train from the opposite direction announced its arrival on the second track. Tanner, no it's Daniel, Henry reminded herself. Daniel stood a little taller and told them he would make the arrangements to take the coffins off the train. Then he went toward a scruffy man with a full white beard standing by a buckboard watching as the train came to a stop.

Jenna leaned over saying, "That's Shorty, he's been acting as the ranch foreman for about five years now. He's been with us since before I can remember so I think he'll be staying."

"Is there a possibility your ranch hands will leave? Have they said so?" asked Henry, thinking someone was jumping the gun. There wasn't any reason to think everything would change now that Mr. Tanner was dead. "Let's wait before we worry, Jenna. Your brother is a tough character. Both your brothers are, I can tell. It's too soon to be making any changes and I know Tan, Daniel, would agree." She watched the signs of strain on Jessie's face relax a little.

"I'm going to go and help lift them, put them in the wagon," Jessie told them gruffly, trying to keep any emotion out of his voice.

Henry and Jenna stepped closer together and watched as the baggage handlers opened the train's sliding door and pushed a coffin out so the men, Tanner, Jessie, and Shorty, on the ground could take the weight on their shoulders and slide it into the waiting wagon. Then the second one was slid out and carried the same way to the wagon to rest next to the first. Jessie pulled a blanket over the coffins and there was a discussion.

"I want to go with Mama and Dad," Jenna said, taking a step toward the wagon.

"Let's go together. You should be able to ride in the wagon if that's what you want. I'm sure we can work out something." The two women went down the steps to the dusty street along the train tracks.

Shorty looked up as the two young women approached. "This must be Danny's little woman. I'm Shorty, nice to make your acquaintance."

"How do you do? I'm sorry this meeting wasn't under happier circumstances." She turned to her husband whose face was granite-like, much as Jessie's was. "Jenna wants to ride with her parents back to the ranch. Would there be room?" Henry asked appealing to Tanner.

Shorty spoke up, "Of course, honey, you can ride right up here with me."

"I'm coming, too," Jessie said, and no one challenged his right to do so.

"I think T, Daniel, should go with you, also. I'll come later by buggy as soon as we can make arrangements," Henry stated getting things organized in her mind.

Shorty nodded. "That sounds 'bout right, Danny. You go with your parents, and I'll drive the little missus out in the buggy. We already got one here. The young 'uns rode out in it while I brought the wagon."

Henry placed her hand on Daniel's arm when she could see he was going to argue that he wouldn't leave her. She said just for his ears, "Take your parents home, Daniel. You should go as a family one last time."

Nodding, he went around and climbed onto the buckboard's bench seat letting Jessie help Jenna up first before following his sister.

Tanner glanced over at Henry, and she nodded encouragingly. "We'll be right behind you. I just need to stop by the general store and pick up some things, but I'll be right behind you."

Tanner picked up the reins tied to the brake and urged the horses into moving, all three riders facing forward, not wanting to remind themselves of their sorrowful cargo.

Henry turned to Shorty as she walked back to the station. "I saw our trunk taken off the train earlier and it's now on the platform. We need to pick that up, and

I'd like to stop and pick up enough food to feed the people who will be coming to the funeral. How many do you think I should plan for?"

"A kind a 'take charge' sort of woman ain't ya?" asked Shorty, his beard hiding whether he was smiling or not.

"I'm afraid I am," confessed Henry as she made mental plans for a menu for the next day.

"I didn't say it was a bad thing, Honey-child. A woman has to take charge sometimes when the men find themselves frozen to the ground. I think you're just what Danny needs in his life," he told her, and this time she saw the smile.

Shorty got to the trunk and hefted it onto his shoulder then led the way to a black two-seated buggy waiting next to the station. Picking up the satchel, she followed the short man hoping everyone at the ranch was as friendly.

Once in front of the store, Shorty told her, "The Tanners were popular ranchers, been in the area since the Comanche were driven out. Warren and Elizabeth were part of the church, the school board, and any town celebration we ever held. There will be upwards about a hundred."

"Oh, that's a lot of people, but I think I can put something together that would be acceptable," she said, multiplying the amounts of things in her mind she had been planning.

Shorty smiled again. "Don't worry, little lady. Didn't I say that the Tanners been very popular and helped every other farmer and rancher in the county, one time or another? Everyone will bring a dish or two plus table service. I'm sure the women here-abouts been making sure they give their friends a good send off. Now if'n you was to add to that, they would be pleased as punch, but it won't be expected. After all, no one knew about you even being here. You'll be a nice surprise. Something good out of something terrible."

"I do feel so sorry for them, all of them. I mean I would have loved to have met both of his parents. Ta, Daniel is being so stoic I don't think it's good for him," she finally admitted her fear out loud.

"I think you're good for him, so I think he'll be all right in the end. The boy's got to grieve some before he can begin to heal."

"I know. I hate to see him hurting, and those poor children, so young to be left on their own." Henry realized if she continued with this kind of thinking she would be a blubbering watering pot in a few moments. "I think I know what I'll need. Do you think the ranch's kitchen is in good shape for food, or do I need to think about meals, also?"

"No, ma'am, the ranch is well stocked, plus we have our own chickens and farm garden, a few fruit trees and beehive. I'll clean some chickens for you and have 'em cut up and ready for the oven in the morning. Anything else you need just say so. I used to be the camp cook during round-ups," he told her proudly.

"Well, I guess I got the best hand out of this deal. I just added a few more dishes to my menu." Climbing down, she entered the store. She wasn't there very long, liking the proprietress who was more than eager to climb ladders and open cases to get what Henry thought she would need.

As the other woman tallied the purchases, she said, "I'll just put this on the ranch's tab. I'll see you tomorrow and, by the way, I'm bringing four berry pies and a few dozen parker house rolls. It was nice to meet you, Mrs. Tanner."

"I'm Henrietta, just plain Henry."

The boy carried out the boxes of food stuff and set them in the back of the buggy while Henry climbed up next to Shorty again. "I'm ready, Shorty, why don't we head for home now?"

Tanner was waiting uneasily on the front porch, climbing down to the dusty drive as soon as Shorty brought the buggy to a stop. "No problems? You're feeling all right?" he asked as he helped Henry down from the buggy.

Henry had a moment to take in the height of the house, first the four steps to the covered porch, then the two-story stucco building above. Big square beams formed the roof line of red-clay tiles and other structural areas.

Taking her arm, he helped her up the steps and through the front door. He led her into a cathedral style room with large stone fireplace taking up one wall, the hearth high enough to comfortably sit on. Several pieces of furniture sat on a colorful rug with geometric designs, and a wide stairway went to the upper level. Quilts hung on the upper hall's walls going to the bedrooms and colorful curtains on the wide room's windows.

"Look, I want you to take a nap and rest, then I'll get you a bath. Do you want any tea? I've got the ginger root with us now," Tanner offered.

"I will take you up on the nap unless Jenna needs me to make supper. Where are they?" she asked glancing around.

"They stayed in the barn with the folks," he said. "I think they need some time to say goodbye in their own way."

"That's probably wise. Is my room upstairs?" She went up the stairs followed by Tanner carrying the carpetbag of necessities.

He opened one of the doors, and she walked into a pleasant room of blue striped rugs and pine log furniture. A washstand and mirror, bureau drawers and large bed took precedence. A large chair in the corner had brightly colored cushions that matched the bed covering and was repeated in the colors of the window's curtains.

Tanner began to empty the bag, placing his shaving kit on the washstand along with his toothpowder. Henry asked, "Is this your room, Tanner?"

"Since I was about five. That's when we moved into the big house. Before that we lived in the ranch hands' bunkhouse. I got the new furniture when I was about twelve. Why?" he asked. "Why are you looking at me like that?"

"Are we to share this room, Tanner? That didn't work out too well the last time we did," she said reasonably.

"I think we're a lot wiser now plus I told you, I won't do anything. You're having my child, and I won't endanger either of you." Then he explained, "There's only the four rooms, and I think it's a little too soon to be moving into my parents' room."

"Of course, it is. I wouldn't expect you to do that," said Henry sadly, thinking of anything else they could do when Tanner continued.

140

"My brother and sister think this marriage is a normal relationship. I don't want to add any worry to their lives. If they think I'm not happy or that you'll take their niece or nephew from them too…. I don't know how to explain what happened when I'm not sure myself." He watched her with a lost expression in his eyes and a frown on his mouth.

"Tanner, I can't sleep with you again. Don't pressure me into this. You said you wouldn't, and now you're making me sorry I ever believed you." Feeling so depressed, she almost sagged with weariness.

"I'll set up a mattress on the floor, and I'll sleep there. I never meant for us to share the bed, to be intimate again. Please don't be upset," he begged again.

"I'm too tired to fight, but remember you've broken almost every pledge you've made to me. How will I ever trust you?" she asked as she crawled onto the bed cover and closed her eyes, blocking out her disappointment with Tanner.

A couple of hours later, there was a light tap on the door and Jenna asked, "Henrietta, supper's ready. Do you want to come down and eat with us?"

Henry stared at the ceiling and the shadows playing across it letting her know the day was almost gone.

"I'll be right down, but I'm not very hungry. I guess I'm not a good traveler," she fabricated. She lay there thinking about what she had gotten into and finally felt she could move without feeling sick. Getting off the bed, she found water in the pitcher, which she used to wash-up.

Once in the kitchen, the table was empty, only Jenna there waiting for Henry. "Everyone else eat then?" asked Henry.

"Yes, they have things they want to get done before tomorrow, making sure everything is neat and clean after the last few days. Jessie's been distracted, and Shorty's been trying to keep us all together. I know he appreciates Daniel coming home like this. I suppose we've interrupted your honeymoon? I know you haven't been married very long," Jenna said as she poured hot water over the dishes in the sink.

"No, you didn't interrupt anything and, of course, Daniel was going to come home to be with you both. He cares for you very much, and although he's being strong, I think he's taking this loss very hard. We're both here for you and Jessie. Let's get through this next day or two then worry about the future."

"I'm trying. I'll be better tomorrow because Eli will be here." Jenna peeked up shyly. "Eli and I have been seeing each other. He's asked for my hand, but Dad wanted us to be a little older and for Eli to be more settled in his job."

"I'll look forward to meeting him, and so will Daniel." Henry searched around saying, "Where are your largest pans? I want to bake a couple of things to add to what the other women will be bringing."

"They're hanging in the pantry over here. The root vegetables are under there, too, and you can get to them from outside if it's easier than climbing down the narrow ladder. Ma always sent me." A tear rolled out from under the young girl's closed lids.

"Oh, Jenna, that's going to happen off and on for a while. Something's going to trigger a memory, and you're going to respond to it. Hopefully they are all good memories." Henry patted her on the shoulder as she passed by on the way to the pantry.

Henry sent Jenna off to bed, preferring the kitchen to herself, a method she often used when she was thinking things out. Cook or bake something then give it away. She had just finished the layer cake with marmalade frosting and was waiting for the peach cobbler to finish baking. A glazed applesauce spice sheet cake was already cooling on the table.

Tanner came in, his hair wet from his washing up on the back porch. "I thought you'd be sleeping. What are you doing here? It's almost dark." He put the tip of his finger to the frosting and quickly into his mouth before she could slap him.

"I wanted to fix a couple of things for tomorrow. I'm a little worried, though. I could only find twenty plates, and I was told to expect a lot more people than that," she said, her brows brought together, trying to concentrate on the funeral luncheon rather than the emotional upheaval Tanner and his siblings were going through. Something she felt at a loss to ease or help with.

"The neighbors will bring some with them, too. You didn't have to worry about the food. I should have told you," he said picking up her hand, playing with her fingers.

"It's something I wanted to do, and it keeps me from fretting."

"But not enough to stop you from fretting over the number of plates we have." He smiled as she acknowledged the truth. "The bunk house has more, and Shorty will bring them out in the morning." Then changing the subject asked, "Did you get time to get a bath? We have an indoor tub and everything."

"I'll take one as soon as I get the cobbler out. It's

almost browned, then I'm done for tonight."

"Then you're done, you mean. I don't expect you to work especially as you're…"

Henry interrupted him. "Don't say it, please. I want to keep that secret until I can make up my mind as to how to handle this. I don't want to meet these people and have them ask personal questions I'm not prepared for."

"See, you're tired and getting cranky. Let me help you with your bath. I can help rinse your hair," he offered provocatively.

"Hush, really Tanner, you are pushing your luck with me tonight." She took a dry towel to take the cobbler out of the oven and let the stove's coals cool down for the night.

"My dad often helped my mother in her bath. Something us kids would pretend we didn't know about as we got older. A lot of giggling went on behind that closed door, and it wasn't always my mother giggling," he told Henry, staring at her. "I love to see you blush."

"Oh, that isn't true. You're making that up to get into my bath. Just stay out here or I'll find a way to make your life miserable," she said, picking up her nightclothes and robe she had brought down earlier.

Tanner's face dropped its smile. "You have the power, Henry. I was just hoping you wouldn't use it."

Entering the bathing room off the kitchen, she lit the lamp on the stand. "I hope I won't have to." Then she shut the door. The water, coming from pipes hanging from the ceiling, was so hot Henry added some cold as well. She luxuriated in the tub, soaping and rinsing her hair twice, finally getting the travel soot out.

Tanner was awake when she got up to their room

although the rest of the house was quiet. Henry didn't want to have an argument and was grateful when Tanner made himself comfortable on the mattress between the bed and the window.

"Good night, Henry," he said into the darkness after she turned out the lamp.

"Good night, Tanner."

CHAPTER TEN

Henry woke up facing an empty mattress on the floor. Tanner already out early either unable to sleep or eager to finish the work from the day before. Going down to the kitchen, she noticed the coffee had been made, but nothing else seemed touched. Putting on her apron, she took out the peas she bought the day before to shuck, getting them ready to cook later, adding pearl onions and butter. She went to locate the potatoes and was surprised to find them already peeled and soaking in cold water. She cut them in bite sized pieces after placing bacon and onion in a large pan to fry.

Shorty came in with buckets of plucked chicken cut up into portions. "These just need a little rinse and seasoning. I did the potatoes earlier so you will have a jump on the meal like we discussed. Anything else I can do for you?"

"Tanner thought you might have more plates and flatware? I could use them if you do. And another coffee pot," she added, thinking of all the things she wanted to cover yet that morning before the service.

If he was surprised, she referred to her husband as Tanner, the older man didn't say anything, but answered, "I'll bring them over. The men are bringing out the tables and benches we use during round-up. And the neighbors will bring benches and chairs, too.

They're a good bunch around here. Don't worry that they won't take care of us," he explained much as Tanner had told her.

"Since you are both so sure, I'll try to relax then. I'll make the dressing for the German potato salad and see what else needs to be done. Do you know where Tanner is?"

"Just outside, ma'am. You need him?" Shorty asked as he turned to leave.

"No, I don't want him to work just to keep from feeling things. He'll have to get ready soon, too," she said realizing she should take her own advice.

Henry stood facing the bedroom window, noticing the noise level downstairs increase. Not having any suitable mourning clothing, she brushed down the skirts of the apricot flowered sprigged muslin she chose to wear on this warm day. The dress had a scoop collar and elbow length sleeves that would meet the lace gloves she had in the sash tied at her still trim waist, the flounces around the hemline rippling with every step. She wore her half boots since they would be walking to the interment.

A couple of hours later, after an unplanned nap, the sound of wagon and buggy wheels filled the front yard and drive. Henry came downstairs to find strangers in the kitchen and a bright white cloth covering the elegant wood-top dining table piled with plates and glasses.

A woman about the age Tanner's mother would have been stopped and smiled when she saw Henry. "You must be Daniel's bride, Henrietta. I'm so glad to meet you though I would have it be under any other condition than this." She blinked back the tears. "I'm Ethyl Mayberry, Elizabeth's oldest friend. I hope you don't mind, but this kitchen is as familiar to me as my own."

"Thank you all for helping like this. I don't think I could have done it by myself," Henry admitted as she continued to the kitchen. The chicken, which Henry had already seasoned with sage, lemon, and parsley was going into the oven. The potatoes had been drained and were cooling. Other pans and pots were on the stove to keep warm or finish cooking. Two other ladies looked up from their jobs and were introduced as Mary Johnson, a woman Ethyl's age, and Emily White, a woman about the same age as Henry, only very big with child.

"I moved here a few years ago, and Elizabeth adopted me and my husband, Seth. Since then I've a three-year-old and one due in a couple of months. Elizabeth was my midwife. I'm going to miss her guidance and strong shoulder." Emily moved the pickles she was slicing to the side and began cutting the fresh tomatoes next. "I might have headed back to my parents years ago if it hadn't been for her. She explained how to make a strong marriage, how to know when to say something, and when to simply stand beside your man. My mother never gave such good advice for me. I can pass it on to you if you want, but with Daniel you may not need the help," Emily said as she kept working alongside the others.

Then Ethyl shooed Henry out of the kitchen saying, "You've done enough. These cakes look delicious, and I'm going to have a big piece of that layer cake. Elizabeth would have been right beside me for a slice of that one."

Henry went to the front window and saw the long tables and benches Shorty had told her about. There were other chairs out on the porch and around other tables that must have arrived with the mourners. Men were standing around talking and shaking hands with each other as they all collected together using this time to meet up with other neighbors. Jessie was out there in a suit with new ten-gallon hat and polished boots, but it was Tanner who took her breath away.

Her husband was wearing a city suit, as Henry always thought of them. Dark brown with tan vest and white shirt topped by a black tie wrapped and tied with a number of folds. A gold watch chain crossed his chest, and he leaned on one foot resting on a chair bottom, the polished boots in plain sight, the spurs gleaming in high style.

His dark blond hair was uncovered at the moment, but she could see his tan Stetson nearby on a table. A slight smile on his face greeted old friends as he shook their hands, an easy way about him. He was the most handsome man Henry had ever seen, and a wave of pride rushed through her as she realized he was hers, all hers, if she wanted to claim him.

Feeling out of place, she went upstairs and sat on the now made bed feeling the edge of the mattress pushed under it. She didn't want to be here at the ranch, but knew Tanner needed her and, in a way, Jenna and Jessie did, too. Pulling herself together, pushing down the nausea she went out to greet the mourners who were still arriving.

Finding Tanner and his siblings on the porch, she stood to his other side and nodded as the people were introduced to her, knowing she wouldn't remember their names afterward there were so many. Shorty was right, the Tanners were well liked, and people were genuinely sad at their passing. Henry hoped their children could take solace in that fact.

The Reverend Mayfield came up to Tanner whispering in his ear, and she saw Tanner firm his lips and nod. Then the minister announced, "Folks, the family and I are going to accompany the coffins out to the grave site where we will hold a ceremony and prayer for the departed. All are welcome to join us."

Since that was what the people had come for, they all waited for the family to file past them while they lined up mostly two by two and followed behind quietly, some of the ladies holding hankies to their eyes as they grieved the passing of their friends. Henry gave an extra handkerchief to both Jenna and Jessie and one for Tanner, too. Someone had given Jenna a bouquet of yellow roses, freshly picked that morning, but already showing the result of the heat.

The wagon was covered with a bright blanket before the coffins were placed inside and it led the way. Shorty, leading the horses to the fenced cemetery a short distance from the back yard where there was already a grave dug, just one and Henry realized the parents were going to be together forever.

She swallowed. The tears were very close to the surface, and she was trying to be strong for Tanner and Jenna, but it was getting more and more difficult. The reverend waited as Tanner, Jessie, Shorty, and two other ranch hands carried first one then the second coffin in and set them on the ropes spread out on the ground next to the grave. Then the minister proceeded followed by Henry and Jenna and the rest of the procession.

When everyone who could crowded into the little cemetery plot, the others remained outside the fence to observe. Tanner stepped forward and began to speak.

"Losing my parents so suddenly made me realize how much they were a part of my life even though I had long been out of the nest and on my own or so I thought. Their passing makes me wish there was one more hunting trip, one more round-up, one more time sleeping together around the campfire, even one more family dinner. But it's too late for any of those one mores, so I'm here to tell you, my friends and neighbors, that don't pass up those 'one mores'. Live every day the way you want the people you care about to remember because it just might be the last time you see them."

Many people nodded in agreement, and murmurings of Amen were heard as Tanner continued, "They spent the best part of their lives together and although we all miss them, I know this is the way they would have asked to go—together. Neither one would have wanted to outlive the other. So, instead of grieving for their loss, we should rejoice in their life and the time they shared with us. And know they are peaceful and together now in death as they always were in life." He stepped back to stand alongside the family he had left.

The reverend stepped forward and said quietly to Tanner only, "I couldn't have said it better, son." Then began his eulogy and prayer. "As they were in life side by side, I lay Warren and Elizabeth Tanner side by side for all eternity. Let us remember them fondly and let those memories bring us joy not sadness. Though we walk through the valley of death..."

Henry couldn't remember much of the rest of the service. She remembered dropping soil on top of the coffins and being led away by a quiet Tanner, no Daniel, she must start thinking of him as Daniel. She is his wife, and his siblings would think it odd if she called him by his last name, well her last name now, too. Oh, when did it get so complicated? She only needed to hang on for another few hours, then the mourners would be gone and she could start to think about the future. Only a few more hours.

Once she was back at the house, Ethyl took over the serving of the luncheon with several other neighbors helping, and soon everyone had a plate full of food and was sitting at the tables or on the porch. Henry refrained from eating anything in case it set off a bout of heaving. Tanner held a cup of coffee and kept milling around from person to person, letting them pay their respects while he thanked them for coming.

If Henry had a dime for every time she heard the phrase, "Daniel, it's been a while. Too bad it couldn't be under happier circumstances..." she'd be a rich woman. Tanner kept being reminded he hadn't been around much, had lost track of the neighbors and what was occurring at the ranch. Jessie ate and talked with several of the younger members of the group, other young men working toward manhood.

Jenna sat next to a young man who must be her future intended. Henry watched as the young man tried to make Jenna smile, held her hand under the table, and patted her shoulder whenever she began to tear up. Henry decided she liked him. Eli, she remembered Jenna saying his name was. He was very attentive and probably would make a good husband even if they were young.

All of a sudden, there was a cold glass of sweetened tea in her hand. Someone with access to ice on this hot summer day had brought some out to the ranch. It had been added to the lemonade and tea and been very welcome on this hot afternoon.

She placed it against her forehead first before drinking any, and to her surprise it tasted good as well as didn't make an immediate reappearance to embarrass her in front of everyone.

Tanner leaned down saying softly, "If you need to go rest, I'll make your excuses. I mean, we just had a long trip getting here. They'll understand." His behavior reminiscent of Eli's toward Jenna.

"It will only be a few more hours, and I'll help with the clean-up. I'm actually feeling pretty good considering," she told him and let him kiss her forehead before leaving her side.

Tanner stopping by her chair didn't go unnoticed, and Emily pulled hers closer saying, "When things have settled down, we should get together. Elizabeth and I used to share recipes. I'd come here or she would come to my place, and we'd make something then split it so we both had supper prepared by the end of the afternoon. It gets kind of lonely. Well, you'll have Jenna of course, but the number of women isn't very many around here, and we're spread out. I could pick you up for church if you'd like."

"I, I'll let you know. I have to get back to my farm to close things up," Henry told her new friend honestly. "We didn't take time to do any of those kinds of things."

"Of course, this caught everyone unprepared. They seemed so young, so full of life." Emily became quiet before saying more robustly, "I promised myself I was over the crying and I am. To change the subject, let me tell you there are several women not so happy to see Tanner married. But some of them are young enough to look toward Jessie, and that young man is going to be as gorgeous as his big brother."

Emily laughed at Henry's raised brows. "Oh, I'm married not dead. I can admire another rancher's stock and not rustle and brand it. Besides, I'm happy with my own man as anyone can see." She patted her protruding stomach so that Henry did laugh out loud.

Encouraged by her success, Emily continued sotto voice, "I love children, I love being with child, and I love getting with child. After all, the winters in Texas can be long and cold." Then she laughed at her own audacity of saying such things to practically a stranger.

"I'll keep that in mind if I'm here during the winter." Then could have bitten her tongue when Emily grabbed on to that piece of information.

"Isn't Tanner staying? Doesn't he plan on continuing just like his dad? Jessie's too young to live here by himself," Emily said concerned.

"I don't know for sure. He hasn't made up his mind yet that I know of, and like I said, I was going to return to my farm and close it up, probably get it ready to sell. All I know is that Ta, Daniel is still part of the Rangers." Then she excused herself since the tea seemed to want to make a reappearance and Henry had to get to a place where such an action wouldn't be seen by all.

Henry's departure from the table seemed to signal

some kind of exodus because soon people were packing up while saying their goodbyes. Henry kept the tea down, after all, and waved from a chair on the porch as buggies and wagons stacked with tables and chairs left the gate and turned either way on the road outside the ranch gate.

Finally, Ethyl came out, her hat placed properly on her head and the white apron folded in her hand. "There's plenty of leftovers to feed you for more than a week. Sorry, no layer cake. That went quickly. Call on me if you need anything or just a shoulder to lean on. I'm glad to have met you. Elizabeth would have loved you. I can tell you that much," the no-nonsense woman said, then yelled for her husband who appeared out of nowhere and they left, too. The last non-Tanner at the house.

"Now will you go and rest? This must have been exhausting for you. I know I'd like to do nothing more than sleep right now, and Jenna seemed washed-out. I already sent her to her room," Tanner told her, as he helped pull her up then pushed her toward the door.

"I will if you will," Henry told him seeing the circles beneath his eyes and the paleness of his skin.

He looked at her, weighing what she said then told her, "I'll be right up. I need to tell Shorty something, then I think it's late enough for bed. The sun is beginning to set so we can call it a day."

Henry took care of the necessary things and changed into her muslin nightgown, sliding between the sheets more out of habit than the need to stay warm. The day had been exhausting both mentally and physically for Henry, and the last thought before she fell asleep was—I hope it gets easier.

Part way through the night, Henry was woken by Tanner lying down on the bed next to her. He tried not to disturb her, but she moaned and woke enough to ask, "Can't sleep?"

"Shhh, I don't want to wake you, just needed to be close enough to hear you breathing. I guess I'm feeling kind of alone now that the funeral's over and I can't go out and talk to them in the barn," he admitted to the darkness.

"You can still go talk to them where they are. I saw Eli and Jenna out there right before everyone began to leave. She's going to have a tough time of it. I was reminded of how desolate it can seem for a woman out here, and she was used to having your mother to talk with," Henry murmured into Tanner's chest.

"I know, and Jessie's mad all the time, and I don't think it's only because I'm here. I mean, it might simply be an age thing, but he seems like he needs to blow-up at something and I'm not sure I want to be the target. How do we recover from something like that? Especially if I win?"

Henry could hear the frustration in his voice. "Try not to be confrontational. Don't boss him around, and don't make any changes to the way the ranch is run. Remember your dad probably put in place all those things, and by changing them you're taking away a little more of your dad each time," she explained her theory.

"How did I get so lucky as to have a smart woman like you as a wife? Did you learn all that in medical school?" he teased pulling her closer to him and moaned as he couldn't prevent himself from kissing her.

156

Henry responded as she always did to his passion. It was involuntary, and her back arched to make it easier to accept his kiss. Tanner brought his hand up to cover a breast, and Henry pulled away.

Tanner put his head down, forehead to forehead, saying, "I'm sorry, I just needed to be close. I know I promised not to do anything."

Henry brushed his hair back from his face explaining, "It's not that, I'm just very sensitive, sore right now."

"Then I'll be careful." He pulled her slowly into his arms to give her time to pull away if that was what she wanted, but she didn't. Henry wanted to share Tanner's pain, help him through this part of his grieving, and give him some of her strength to go along with his own. Help him through this first night of the rest of his life.

Returning his kisses, she left his mouth and trailed her lips down his neck and over his chest, licking the salt that she tasted there hearing his indrawn breath as she did so.

"Henry," he said breathlessly. "Henry, stop! I think I better go back to my mattress. I can't, I can't handle this, too."

"Don't worry, I can do all the work," she said as she found the top of his trousers already partially unbuttoned for comfort and knew his arousal was just beneath her hand.

"I want you so much, but I don't want to hurt you or the baby. Maybe we should wait," he said agonizingly slowly as he let her hand slide over his erection and he relaxed his body against hers. She tugged his trousers lower.

Henry whispered as she threw her leg over his now naked hips, "You won't hurt me or the baby. It's well protected believe me." Then she pressed down and encased him within her warmth.

Another moan, but this time of pure bliss as she felt her thighs touch both his sides and he arched his hips in a natural supplication for more. Henry smiled raising herself enough to slide down him and repeated the process, feeling the center of the hurricane begin to spread out and encompass more of her body, giving her little tastes of the finale. Holding back enough so that she kept her movements long and slow.

As the momentum increased, so did Tanner's need for her, his hands now on her hips as he helped set the pace and the angle until she felt the coil of ecstasy begin to unwind. Tanner began to groan and call her name, and Henry placed her hand lightly over his mouth, reminding him Jenna and Jessie were just across the hall.

Both of them stiffened, Henry throwing her head back and feeling her toes curl before finally succumbing to the culmination of feelings and lights and release that made her collapse on top of him with a soft cry of, "Daniel," as she tried to catch her breath.

Sliding off, she pulled her gown down to cover her nakedness as Tanner pulled her close to his body whispering, "I'm sorry. I promised…Now you'll hate me again."

Stroking his chest, he fell into a much-needed deep sleep as she knew he would. "No, don't worry about that. I won't hate you." Then thought—but I will hate myself in the morning.

CHAPTER ELEVEN

Henry found herself alone in the bed, alone in the room, when the sun came up enough to light the corners. She hoped Tanner hadn't been up for long since he needed the sleep, and for what he had to face during the next few days he needed to be well rested. Getting the ranch business settled was going to be touchy. Jessie wasn't likely to take orders from Daniel now their father was gone. But in truth, Jessie was too young to have all the responsibility piled on his shoulders alone.

Dressing, she pinned up her hair into a simple bun then went downstairs to find the kitchen empty of people. She wasn't really hungry but thought she should try to eat something every day in case the nausea was gone. She opened some of the covers in the cooler pantry and pie safe, but nothing seemed interesting until she came to a rice dish she didn't remember seeing the day before. It looked like mostly chicken and rice, and it smelled kind of spicy. She took a spoonful and placed it on a saucer and took it outside to the porch in case her stomach rejected it too quickly for her to react.

To her pleasant surprise, her stomach didn't recoil. She actually felt hungry, so she got another couple of spoonsful of the jalapeño laced casserole. She didn't know why, but she seemed to tolerate this food when

159

any other time she would have needed a couple of glasses of water to eat it.

She didn't hate herself as much as she thought she would about making love with her husband, but she was disappointed with herself. Now after days of telling Tanner they didn't have a chance of being together she made love to him as if she couldn't get enough of him. And last night, she couldn't.

It must have something to do with being with child. Henry never thought she would feel so sensitive to his every movement inside her, excited by the very thought of his being in her. She hoped, like the nausea, this too would pass after the three-month mark was over.

Tanner came into the kitchen warily, unsure of his welcome. "You feeling all right?"

She knew he asked to make sure what they did last night didn't have a negative effect on her or the baby even though she had told him it wouldn't.

"I'm fine, well, maybe better than fine. I ate some of whatever this is, and it seems to be staying down. But about last night, don't plan on doing that again. I shouldn't have begun it, and I certainly shouldn't have finished it." She felt better after taking the blame before he could be chivalrous and apologize to her. "I don't blame you at all, you didn't do anything."

"No, darlin', I was doin' something. I wasn't so tired I didn't know what we were doing." He smiled his understanding. "But you can take the lead anytime you like."

"Last night didn't change anything, Tanner. I'm still planning on moving on, where ever that may be. As soon as things are settled here, I need to sell my farm and get on with my life, start all over."

"If you stayed with me, there wouldn't be that much to do. You could keep the farm and pay Jason to take care of it if you wanted. The longer I'm here the more I find I wouldn't feel comfortable leaving Jessie alone. Jenna is almost married, and he'll be alone most of the time. Even with Shorty helping, Jessie's still not old enough to take over the ranch," he told her, showing his worry over his younger brother.

A young male voice yelled from the doorway. "That's just what I thought you'd do. Put your big nose into my life. Dad thought I was old enough to leave it in my care when he went to San Francisco so who are you to tell me I'm not ready?"

"Dad thought he was only going to be gone a few weeks. Things have changed, Jessie. I'm not putting my nose in your business, this ranch belongs to Jenna and me, too, now. We'll all vote on how to run things just as we always have," Tanner told his younger brother face to face, not backing down, but appearing to confront Jessie at a level Jessie couldn't compete on.

Henry tried to touch Tanner, make him see how threatening his pose seemed. Henry didn't think Tanner would hurt Jessie, not unless Jessie attacked, but that might happen if Tanner didn't back down.

Her message must have gotten to him because he deflated, relaxing the muscles in his neck and arms saying, "It isn't what I meant, Jessie. I just mean all of us need to figure out how not to dump the burden of taking care of the ranch on your shoulders. You deserve some help around here. After all, it used to take both you and Dad to run things, and Shorty is getting older, he isn't as quick to move around anymore."

The more reasonable tone of voice should have

soothed Jessie's ruffled feathers, but it didn't seem to. He was hiding behind his anger, keeping the tears from falling. The young man turned around and strode to the barn.

"That didn't go well. I don't know how to talk with him anymore. I told you he seems angry at me all the time. I guess it's been too long since we just sat around and talked. I spent most of my time here with Dad when I visited. I didn't know what to say to Jenna, and Mom was always Mom. We spoke at dinner and a little in the evenings, but mostly about my life outside the realm of the Rangers. You know, do I meet any proper young ladies and will I ever give her any grandbabies." He smiled over at Henry, insinuating she had covered both his mother's wishes.

"He just lost his compass. He doesn't have another male to look to for strength. He's afraid to show weakness to you since he thinks you'll use it against him. You shouldn't try to take the place of your father, but you need to take the place of a strong male who Jessie can feel he can depend on," Henry explained.

Tanner asked, "How do I go about doing that? I mean, not be Dad, but replace him in Jessie's life?"

"Gently and slowly. Let him get to know you again, let him see the similarities between you and your dad, because from what I heard yesterday you two were very alike. That alone might be intimidating to him, the odd man out so to speak. Now he'll never be able to prove to your dad he is as good as you are, that he'll remain loyal to the ranch which you didn't." She rubbed his shoulders easing the tenseness out of them.

"I'll try to speak with him again tonight after supper. Maybe if we get back into a normal schedule he'll see that I don't want to take anything from him. I just want to help. I know how hard running a ranch can be, and I don't want Jessie feeling it's all been dumped on him now." He sounded frustrated as he went back out to help Shorty.

It was late in the afternoon while Henry was baking bread in the kitchen with Jenna when they heard Shorty yelling for help, calling Danny's name. "Danny, I need help. Jessie's been hurt. I need help."

Both Jenna and Henry ran out the backdoor dreading what they would see after the warning from the older man. He was leading Jessie's horse, the young man barely holding on to the saddle horn, trying not to collapse onto the ground. Jessie's left side was covered in blood and his arm hanging uselessly on his thigh.

At the same time the women came out of the house, Daniel ran out of the barn rushing to the side of Jessie's horse and pulled him off gently. He held Jessie in his arms and worriedly turned toward Henry just as Shorty was saying, "We need to get him into town and hope the doc isn't out on a call. I found him all tied up in wire. The damn fool kid was trying to string wire by his self. He knows better than that. It's always a two-man job for just this reason."

Everyone could see Shorty was mad at himself for not realizing what Jessie had been doing.

Henry snapped into action ordering, "Daniel, carry him in and put him on the dining table. Jenna, put that blanket from the back of the couch on the table ahead of him, and I'll need some water in a bowl with clean cloths. Shorty, I'll need you to help hold Jessie down while I do the sutures. I'll get my bag from upstairs."

No one questioned her right to give orders, and

Daniel told her he'd get the bag while she began getting Jessie cleaned up. Jenna stood to the side, worried eyes and trembling lips, but she held the tears at bay until there was a real reason to cry. At least Jessie was still alive. They could tell by his pain-filled moans every time he was moved.

"Jenna, find that bottle of whiskey I saw the other day in the breakfront and pour some in a small bowl and a goodly amount in a glass for your brother."

Henry took the pair of scissors and began cutting the shirt material off Jessie, thanking his thinking ahead when he put on the leather vest before going out to work that morning. Some of the blood was already dried which meant Jessie had probably lain out in the hot sun for hours before being found.

"Jessie, can you hear me?"

He opened his pain-filled eyes, nodding.

"Do you drink?" As he shook his head, Henry said, "You will today. It will help with the pain."

"Daniel, help Jessie drink that down and give him a little more if you think he isn't drunk enough," Henry told him as he came into the room.

Daniel had returned with the medical bag that was in the trunk from the farm. Opening it, Henry took out the needles and thread she was going to use to do the suturing and placed them in the bowl of alcohol. Washing some of the injured arm, she found the sliced skin surrounded by multitudes of little cuts caused by the razor-sharp barbs on the wire to keep the cattle from brushing against the fencing and pushing it over.

Washing and making sure there were no threads from his shirt caught in the wound caused the bleeding to begin again. Jenna made a little whimper when she saw it. Henry finished the cleansing and let her fingertips slip into the bowl alongside the needles for a couple of minutes.

Threading the curved needle, she began a methodical suturing, the deepest most dangerous cuts first then attention to the smaller ones that bled less profusely.

It was a tedious job. Shorty and Daniel, one on each side, kept Jessie from fighting her or moving as she stitched his arm and side under the vest where the wire had wrapped itself around his vulnerable body. Covering the wounds with a salve, she looked over her handiwork, satisfied. Finally, Henry stood up stretching then rubbed her eyes, which she had been straining for the last hour.

Jessie was snoring softly, and she smiled saying, "Well, at least we know he's a quiet drunk. He'll simply find a corner and fall asleep whenever he gets too much. Can you get him up to his bed?" She looked questioningly at Daniel, who nodded then lifted his brother for the trip up the stairs.

"I'll go and make sure his bed is open for him," Jenna said, taking her brother's boots and vest with her as she hurried upstairs before Daniel got there with his burden.

Glancing outside, Henry was surprised to see it was dark and the bread dough risen over the sides of the pans in the kitchen. She put it into the oven, which was still hot, and sat down again to wait for them to bake.

Daniel came back downstairs saying wearily, "I need coffee. Can I get you something?"

She shook her head wondering about how she could go to sleep in the middle of the kitchen and not let the bread burn.

"I guess the family discussion is off for this evening, so have you made any decisions since I left you this morning?" Daniel asked seemingly afraid of her answer.

"I'll have to stay around for a few more days at least to take out the stitches and make sure Jessie doesn't get any infections. Wire is known to carry some of the worst," she stated, noting Daniel's shoulders relax when he heard her answer. "But this doesn't mean I'm staying, only postponing my leaving. I wouldn't abandon your family when anyone was in need."

"I appreciate your doing this because I know it isn't something you want to be associated with anymore. It would have taken hours to get Jessie to the doctor or the doctor here if we could find him. He's very busy covering the whole county. You took care of Jessie immediately, and I know he's in a lot more comfort than he would have been." Tanner smiled then sniffed the air. "Is that bread baking?"

"Jenna and I were just finishing the bread when Jessie got here. It's not perfect, but we'll make more tomorrow if it's too bad. We can always use this for stuffing or bread pudding. I just didn't want to waste it," Henry told him covering a yawn.

"Go upstairs, now. You're tired, and I can wait for the bread. Is there anything I should do for Jessie when he wakes up?" he asked as she headed upstairs.

"Yeah, get me and I'll make sure everything is healing as it should," she shot back at him.

Henry undressed, pulling on her gown without lighting the lamp, and climbed into her bed. She wasn't hungry, but she was exhausted and soon fell asleep hearing Jenna talking to someone, but it wasn't Jessie, not yet. She must have stopped Daniel from coming to bed and Henry fell asleep.

The next morning, Henry found the rice and jalapeño dish and ate some again, keeping it down, so she added some bread in her optimism. She made tea with sugar and felt decent for the first time in weeks. Jenna came down with a tray she evidently had taken to Jessie.

"He said he wasn't hungry when I checked on him earlier, so did he eat anything?" Henry asked her sister-in-law. Funny, that was the first time she thought of Jenna as a sister.

Jenna showed her the empty dishes. "Ate every bite so he must be feeling better, right?"

Smiling, Henry continued making her tea when Jenna asked, "How did you know Daniel was the right one for you?"

Henry took a moment to figure out what to say, and Jenna must have thought she hadn't understood the question. "I mean, did you know at first sight like my parents or did it take a while? When did you meet?"

"It's complicated, like all relationships, I guess," Henry prevaricated. "I was attracted to him almost from the beginning. After all, he's a good-looking man, but, no, I didn't think I was in love."

"Then did you get funny feelings inside or see a bright light or something that told you he was the one, the one you wanted to live the rest of your life with?" Jenna asked almost frantically.

"Jenna, what's this really about? Do you have doubts about Eli or is he pressuring you to make a decision or to do something you're not ready for?" Henry had never felt like a mother more than at that moment.

"No...well, kind of. He wants us to marry so I can go and live with him in town and not be out here alone. I'm sure part of it is so we can, um, be together you know, but he's also worried about me. He knows the men are gone most of the time especially in the spring during round-up. With winter coming, there will be days when he won't be able to come out to visit me at all."

The young girl turned with a worried expression. "Eli says you and Daniel aren't planning on staying. He said Daniel will need to get back to the Rangers or lose his job since there are more than enough men wanting those positions."

"Well, there is only one reason to get married, and that's because you love that person so much you can't see yourself living without them. If or when you feel that for a man, then you'll know whether he's the right one or not," Henry told the younger woman easily now she herself found the true answer within her own heart.

"So, that's what it's like for you and Daniel? You love each other so much you had to be together?" Jenna asked innocently.

"Yes, something like that, but we were discussing you and Eli. You have plenty of time to make up your mind, and if Eli isn't the one then tell him you're not sure. If he loves you, he'll wait, and if he won't wait, then he wasn't the right one in the first place."

"You make it sound so easy. No wonder Daniel loves you. I would have taken weeks to boil it all down and still worried if I was doing the right thing." Jenna hugged Henry to her then finished, "Thank you, you're the best sister ever."

Daniel helped Jessie down the stairs to use the privy. The young man stayed downstairs for supper, eating heartily, evidently his usual amount since Jenna teased him all through the meal about how fast he was eating and how much was being shoveled into his mouth. Daniel smiled at his siblings, and Henry enjoyed watching the family-workings, something she never had as an only child of a widower.

When the meal was over, Daniel helped Jessie go upstairs again, although it was already an un-needed service, but it was letting the brothers bond. Henry felt she wasn't going to be needed much longer here, and she let her mind think of all the things she would need to do. Now she was married she may not have to leave her little farm, simply find someone to live with her to take care of the child when she's called out on an emergency with one of the farmers.

Possibly Jason's oldest sister. After all, she has a lot of experience in childcare, and Jason's mother was very clean so her daughters would be good at that, too. There were so many decisions she fell asleep in the darkening parlor without making any final plans.

Daniel woke her with a kiss saying, "Hey, wake up, sleepy head, time for bed."

"You woke me up to send me to bed? What kind of sense is that?" she complained as she followed him upstairs.

The next day Jenna and Henry began changing the bed linen and gathering laundry. Jessie felt much better, and the stitches were almost ready to be removed although Henry kept reminding him not to scratch at them. She loaned him a couple of her books to keep him entertained while he was stuck in the house. At least he knew he needed to keep away from any source of dirt.

"You can move that arm, don't baby it any longer, but don't do anything that would tear out those stitches. I won't work on you while you're drunk next time. You'll feel every needle prick, and I won't be so neat either. You're going to have very thin lines with these sutures so brag about them while they still show," Henry warned.

"Does that mean I can go to town and show the girls?" he asked teasingly.

"You can go to town in a couple of days when the stitches are out," she answered.

Jenna boiled water in the kitchen pots. Soon the clotheslines were hoisted up on poles to keep the sheets from dusting the ground in the slight breeze that came across the fields. Henry emptied the last boiler full of cooled dirty water on the garden plants and hung it back on the porch. They saw a dust cloud on the main road, and Jenna put her hand over her eyes to see who was in such a hurry, but it wasn't necessary because the buckboard turned into their gate to come to a noisy stop at the front of the house.

Emily's husband was red-faced and worried, his brows down in concern as he said, "Emily's time has come early. I know you aren't experienced, but you're the closest woman, and I don't want to leave her too long." The three-year-old boy in a smocked dress played with the strap on Seth's hat while sitting on his father's lap.

Emily turned to Jenna saying, "Jenna, could you watch this child? I'll send for him when we have his mother taken care of."

"Of course, Samuel and I are great friends. We made cookies when our mothers cooked together." Jenna put her arms up to take the child from his father, who nodded his thanks as he gave him up.

Daniel reached them when he heard the last part. "I'll bring her in a buggy, Seth. She can't be jostled around in a buckboard." A silent message passed between the two men.

Henry turned to get her bag as Daniel told Seth, "Go back to your wife. We'll be right behind you. You won't have to worry, Henry's a licensed physician. She'll be all your wife will need, I'm sure, but I'll send Shorty into town to round up the doctor."

Turning the buckboard around, Seth headed back the way he came while Daniel ran to the barn to get the buggy. Jenna was already playing with Samuel in the parlor when Henry ran through after getting her bag.

"This may be a while so can you put him to bed if we aren't back by then?" Henry asked.

"Sure, he's used to napping on my bed, so we'll be just fine. Good luck with everything." She hesitated as Henry gathered clean towels from the kitchen and asked, "Is it true what Daniel said? That you're a doctor? Is that why you could sew up Jessie, you're not just a veterinarian?"

"I'm a trained doctor, but I prefer working with animals. It's complicated. Oh, there's the buggy, I'll send information as soon as I can." Henry grabbed the pile of linen and her bag and hurried out the door.

The White's farm was smaller and more of a cabin

than a house. Evidently this place was run by Seth alone, and it looked like it was more than he was able to handle with the paddock needing to be cleaned and an air of seediness about the outbuildings.

Daniel drew up to the house, and Henry got down taking the linens and bag with her as she knocked then entered the house. Hearing Emily's cry of pain coming from one of the two rooms divided off by thin walls from the rest of the cabin, Henry strode there quickly.

"Emily, I'm here," she announced herself and entered just as Emily was getting through a contraction.

"Let's see what we have, shall we? Tell me what's happened so far." She listened as she washed while Emily and Seth both filled her in on the backpains and the water breaking about four hours earlier. Because it was so early in her pregnancy, Emily thought it was a mistake. Then Henry checked the progress of the birth and sat back on the bed.

"You are definitely having this baby, probably yet tonight. I don't like the idea this baby is so early, so we'll need to keep a close eye on it," Henry told the worried parents.

"I've never been very consistent so that date really was a shot in the dark. I mean, we had to tell people something so we set the date with the doctor's opinion. It may be closer to eight months than seven," confessed Emily.

"That would be better for the baby, but we'll see after the birth. It's the lungs that form last, so it's important to keep the baby inside for as long as possible, but seven and a half months isn't an impossible time for the baby to live a healthy life. Don't worry, you seem fit and strong, and that is a big help in the health of the infant." Henry tried to leave the parents with something positive.

"Seth, you may stay, it won't bother me, but Emily has a lot of work ahead of her. She might be able to sleep between contractions if you and Daniel stay out of the way. I noticed there was already water cooling on the stove so besides feeding yourselves, I don't think you have a job for a while."

Seth looked at his wife, saying, "I'll go out and keep Daniel company, but call me if you want me in here with you." Then kissed her as he left, showing he was not happy about being sent out of the room even if he hated to see Emily in pain.

Daniel had been pacing in the kitchen, hearing most of what went on in the bedroom in the small cabin. "I noticed you could use a little help with the paddock. I could help you do it if you want to keep your mind off what's going on in here. It seems we have a few hours to wait."

"Yeah, I got a little behind. Emily usually helps out on those things, but she's been so tired, and with this heat she gets exhausted over the littlest things. I take Samuel with me, too, and I have to really watch him. He can get into more trouble than you can imagine," Seth said as they walked out to the small barn, which was really more of a stable.

Along with Daniel's strength, the two men fixed the hanging sliding door and replaced split fence posts in the paddock. Seth cleaned up the dung and put it in the pile behind the building where he was making potential fertilizer for his fields in the fall. The lean-to up against the stable needed shingles replaced, and

Daniel began splitting them, so soon the men's minds were busy with work and less worrying about Emily and Henry.

Daniel tried not to think of Henry being in this same position in a few months. He had heard women's cries during birthing before in his career as a Ranger, but not with anyone he knew. Just knowing Emily was in pain made it so much more real, which meant he would feel even worse when it came Henry's time. He wasn't sure he would be able to forget her being in pain and concentrate on work when her time came as he was trying to do now.

In fact, he didn't think he would leave her side when the baby wanted to make his appearance. He would be there beside her damning himself for making her go through something like that. He had enough guilt about not protecting her when they were in that hotel room when she needed his comfort more than anything. He had felt lucky and grateful and, hell, proud when she offered herself, but the result was that she would be in pain a few months from now.

Preparing things she would need for the newborn, Henry tried to make Emily more comfortable before ordering her to rest, take a nap if she could. The first few hours were quiet, and the men checked on the developments without waking Emily.

Eventually Emily progressed to the point where there wasn't time to take a breath between contractions. Henry positioned herself so she could help guide the infant into the world, but Emily was doing all the work. At least she wasn't worn completely out yet having taken advantage of resting as Henry ordered.

Emily told Seth to stay in the kitchen. She didn't want his hovering to distract her, so Seth and Daniel were there drinking way too much coffee now it was dark outside and there wasn't any work to keep them occupied.

"You're doing just fine, Emily. I can see the crown of the baby, and it's exactly how we like to see it. Push when you get this next one, and yes, just like that. All right, this next one should have you a mother of two." Henry smiled in encouragement knowing the pain and pressure was extreme for Emily at this point.

Gritting her teeth, Emily tried not to cry out in pain. She already explained to Henry she was trying not to drive her husband to distraction. The last push was the magical one, a small baby girl slid out and was wrapped in a receiving blanket. The umbilical cord was cut as Henry announced the gender to the mother.

Henry cleared the breathing passage with a swipe through the small mouth with a finger. Expecting to hear the loud squall of an indignant newborn mad at being removed from its warm cocoon, Henry tapped the infant's feet and swiped her mouth again. Picking up the baby girl and placing her chest against Henry's ear, she couldn't detect a heartbeat or possibly only a faint one.

Fear raced through Henry as she placed the baby on the floor. She covered the baby's mouth and nose with her own, blowing lightly to inflate the newborn's lungs. This couldn't be happening. This child couldn't be lost was a litany that kept going through Henry's mind. She couldn't disappoint another couple, be the cause of a family's loss again. She prayed as she blew the constant little breaths into the infant and rubbed her little heart.

Emily let out a wail for the loss of her baby, assuming it was dead as Henry took the baby out of her sight. Seth ran in going straight to his wife as she cried in anguish, "My baby's dead, oh, Seth, my baby's dead." The new mother broke into heartbreaking sobs.

Daniel was right behind Seth at Emily's cry of grief but went to his wife, who he saw bent over the dead infant crying. He knew a death like this would be devastating to Henry, the reason she no longer wanted to practice as a doctor. This was going to be hard for her to get over, and he wasn't sure how he was going to be able to help her. He kneeled next to her anyway.

"Henry, love, please don't cry. You tried your best. These things happen." He tried to hold her to his body.

Then he realized what she was doing and, although he didn't understand it, he knew she was trying to save the infant. There was a faint gurgling cry and as Henry rolled the baby onto its side, the cry got louder. Loud enough for Emily to hear it, her mouth open in wonder.

Daniel looked up in happy amazement to the parents. "That's your baby, she's crying. I think she's going to be all right. Give Henry a minute and she can tell you herself."

Henry wiped her mouth on her sleeve, leaving a smear of blood there, and picked up the crying infant to hand to her mother. With tears in her eyes, Henry said, "It's a girl and she'll be fine now. I don't think there's anything weak about her lungs. They sound good to me."

After handing the baby girl to Emily, Henry turned into Daniel's chest and cried in relief until the front of his shirt was wet with her tears.

A few minutes later she pushed away from Daniel. "I have to check on Emily. You, Daniel, out of the room. Seth, you can stay, but give her some room."

Both men obeyed immediately, but Emily kept hold of her daughter, afraid to put her down now that she was sure the baby was perfect in every way.

"I can't thank you enough, Henry. If we had been alone, I don't know that we could have saved Violet. I...." She stopped a sob. "I thought she was gone."

"But she's not. She's strong, and I want to make sure she can suckle before I leave you. I'm your house guest for the next few days, and Jenna will keep Samuel until we send for him. I suggest in a couple of days, but don't wait too long. We don't want him to think his sister replaced him in your affections. He needs to know she's an addition not the center of the family," Henry explained as she cleaned up the bed and the room before leaving the new family together.

Once out in the main part of the cabin, Henry dropped her head in a short prayer. Not that she hadn't asked for His help before this, but this one was more of a thank you.

Daniel came to her saying, "Well, I still don't see the doctor, so I guess you being here was important. But let's get you resting. I saw a small bed in the other bedroom, but it's big enough for you. I'll make up a bed for what's left of the night out here and let the ranch know how everything went. I'll cancel the doctor unless you think he needs to be here."

She shook her head. "I'm going to lie down but should check on Emily in an hour or two, so get me then." Lying down, she let her head hit the pillow followed by closed eyes.

The next day was busy for Henry. She washed all the linen that was soiled plus the apron she wore and Emily's nightgown. When Ethyl showed up, the cabin was back to its pristine condition and Emily and the baby were clean and ready for visitors.

Ethyl stated in her forthright manner, "I brought some stew and bread and a few other goodies to help tide you over until Emily is back on her feet. Shorty let us know, so the neighbors have made up a schedule for coming and helping out each day. Emily needs to recoup her strength to care for two small children."

Then turned her attention to Henry. "What about you, Henry? Quite a sly puss you are being a doctor and all and not letting us know."

"I, um, retired from practice. I haven't worked with people for several years. It's just that I was the only one available at the time. Emily did all the work, I simply held out my hands, and there Violet was." Henry laughed at the age-old joke among doctors, at least.

"Don't tell me that. Seth is telling everyone who will listen that you saved his family. You saved this infant when everyone else thought she was dead," Ethyl insisted.

"I did what had to be done. These things happen and I'm so thankful I was there to help Emily," Henry told the older woman, feeling uncomfortable with the praise because Henry was well-aware of what would have happened if the baby had died instead. The blame would have been double any praise she received now. Doctors were supposed to be able to save lives, anything else was unacceptable.

Henry left after two days, the women coming to

care for the house and new mother experienced with both. Daniel seemed happy to be taking her back to the ranch. He had been checking with her each evening but told her it wasn't the same as having her there nearby to talk with. And Jessie's stitches needed to be taken out since he was anxious to get back to work, prove he could handle the ranch on his own.

Out of the blue Daniel asked, "How did you know what to do with that baby? You were pushing on her and breathing for her, weren't you?"

There was a pause before Henry explained, "Where I spent my internship, I worked under a physician who had lost a child from drowning in a pond. The doctor wanted all of us to know this procedure in case we were faced with someone in that condition. It's not new, but I thought if it worked for drowning victims then it might work in this instance, too. The baby was drowning, couldn't get air, so I did the only thing I knew to do."

"And Emily and Seth are deeply grateful you did. I felt so proud of you at that moment, to actually save a life is truly a gift," he told her as they bounced over a rut in the road and he grabbed for her.

"And we were lucky it worked. If underdeveloped lungs were the reason she couldn't breathe, then there wouldn't have been anything I could do. I don't want to be placed in that situation ever again. I'm not strong enough," she confessed.

"I don't think that's true. I saw you that night, and you're strong enough for anything. It's never easy to use untried methods when no others are available. I mean someone tried that procedure with an almost dead person and found it worked. That's all you can expect from yourself, that you tried your best."

He stopped to find the right words. "I'm not telling you to go back to being a doctor. I guess I'm saying if you do, accept the fact you can't save everyone. All you can do is try and if you fail, then make them as comfortable as possible until the end."

Henry became anxious to get out of the buggy as soon as she saw the ranch, everything about it appealed to her, and she didn't want to think too deeply about why. Jenna ran up to her and hugged her, while Jessie met her with the inevitable request to remove the stitches, that they had been killing him with their itchiness. Daniel tried to chase him away, but Henry agreed it was time to remove them. She got the small scissors out of her bag and began the slow process of cutting the many tiny sutures.

Jenna was talking non-stop, telling Henry everything she had been doing the three days Henry had been absent from the ranch. Including how much fun she had with Samuel and asked what the baby, Violet, looked like. And that Ethyl had put Jenna in the schedule to stay at the White's farm. Also, Eli visited every day, well every evening, and was so good with Samuel it made her almost cry seeing them together.

Henry smiled, knowing Jenna needed to unload everything while Henry couldn't stop herself from asking, "Any new thoughts on Eli?"

"I don't know why I felt like I should wait. Eli's been wonderful ever since we heard about Mom and Dad. He hasn't been pressuring me. In fact, he kind of said maybe we should wait a while before we get married so people don't think we did something the parents weren't in favor of. It wasn't Eli, they just thought I needed to be older, but I'm eighteen now and that's how old Mom was when she got married," Jenna said in a rush.

"I'm not the right person you need to convince, Jenna. Your brother is your guardian, I would think, and he isn't unreasonable about these things. You need to speak with him, or you and Eli could together. Possibly have at least a short engagement first." Henry offered her advice after promising herself she wouldn't interfere. Maybe it was harder to keep promises than she thought.

The sun was setting as Tanner came in after supper. "Come with me. I want to show you something." He took her hand and pulled her toward the east porch, the one where she would spend every summer morning drinking tea if this were her home.

There was a rocking chair with a high back and wide arms. Tanner sat down pulling Henry across his lap and he rocked them a little saying, "My parents used to spend quite a bit of time out here in the evenings, especially if they had been having an argument earlier in the day." She could hear the smile in his voice.

"I wouldn't have thought your parents ever disagreed about anything," she said, surprised at his confidence.

"Oh, they disagreed all right about a lot of things, but they always seemed to come to an understanding out here. It's what made their union so strong." He continued to rock, lost in memories, so Henry didn't interrupt his thoughts and watched the moon rise and stars appear instead.

"I can see why being out here could solve a lot of issues. I mean when you look out there you realize how small you are and how much smaller your problems are, especially silly arguments," she finally said out loud not expecting any answer.

"I remember the last big blow-up. Mom practically frog-marched my dad out here and sat him down. They were arguing about my joining the Rangers. Dad wanted me to stay on the ranch and learn more so I could take over. I thought I had learned enough, and I didn't plan on being a rancher. I wanted to see more of the country, more of Texas. By the time they came back in, my dad was happy to let me go, and my mother was happy I would come back and visit them regularly, which I did for the most part. This last time was the longest I'd ever been away, and I feel guilty about that now," he said stroking her hip and down her leg unconsciously.

"They were on a trip themselves when this happened. Don't blame yourself. You don't blame them for going on vacation, do you?" she asked realistically.

Tanner waited a moment then said, "No, they were reliving their meeting one another over thirty years ago. It was in celebration of their anniversary. My mother had been attending a cotillion and my dad, who was a few years older, watched her dance with practically every other man there. She had already booked her dances or something like that, so Dad paid one of the men on her dance card to let him take his place. Ma didn't know all of the men that well, just accepted their request for a dance since only the most uppity ups had been invited. My father wasn't on the invitation list, kind of a gate-crasher I guess you'd call him." Tanner laughed, then continued the story, "He danced with my mother, told her she was going to marry him, and when someone realized he wasn't supposed to be there, got thrown out. But he got my mother's name and address and showed up the next day at her home. Got thrown out of there, too, but they were married less than a month later."

Henry was smiling just thinking of a man much like Tanner doing all of that and knowing the acorn didn't fall far from the tree. "And when is your birthday?"

"I was thirty, three months ago, why?" he asked.

"Because I was thinking how much like your father you are." And buried her head into his chest chuckling as he did the math and realized why she was laughing.

"The Tanner men just know what's good for us. It's our job to prove it to our women." She felt him kiss the top of her head.

"I don't know. Brow-beating is more like it."

"You don't know anything about my mother if you think she could be brow-beat into anything. I felt sorry for my dad because I think she manipulated him something terrible." He stroked down her dress then back up her bare leg, and she grabbed at his hand as it slid under her skirts.

"Tanner, you promised," she admonished.

"I'm not doing anything for me. I'm just petting you. It's to relax you. It's to make you feel good, darlin'," he said in a whisper as he stroked the back of her leg up to her fanny and back to the knee again.

"I don't need relaxing, and I don't need to be petted," she assured him.

Tanner spent some quiet moments ignoring Henry's trying to wiggle off his lap, his hand finding the warm core, his gentle touch inflaming her desire.

"Tanner, you promised," she warned.

"And I meant every word when I said it." He covered her mouth with his, thrusting his tongue in to parlay with hers, holding himself in check as he continued to arouse her. Their kissing continued, both seeking the other while Tanner brought Henry to completion and she could finally breathe freely as he let her rest against his chest.

"See? I kept my promise. I simply pleasured you so you could relax and sleep, darlin'," he told her, petting the inside of her thigh as she caught her breath. "Now you go on up and get to bed. I'll stay down here and cool off a little, maybe sit in the horse trough or something."

"What am I going to do with you, Tanner? You refuse to take this seriously," she said as she got off his lap feeling replete yet frustrated with her husband at the same time.

"I disagree. I'm taking this very seriously, and I'm trying to show you what you're throwing away." His eyes caught the moonlight as he spoke.

Henry turned and walked into the house, wondering if perhaps she was being too set on her original plans to find merit in his.

Tanner found Henry sound asleep when he went in and pulled his mattress out from under the bed. Lying on his back, he listened to her breathing. He would miss that sound if she ever left him. Those nights with her staying at the White's had been torture for him knowing he couldn't stay in the small cabin with the new family as well.

The night of the birth he hated to wake Henry when she had told him to but knew Emily's health probably depended on it. He worried she gave too much of herself to others, but he wouldn't mind her being a little more giving with him. Give him a chance to prove he could be a good husband. Give him a chance to be a good lover. Give him a chance to be a good father.

CHAPTER TWELVE

Henry was torn with her feelings, feelings that grew stronger and stronger toward Daniel, Jenna, Jessie, and even the ranch. She felt comfortable here among her mother-in-law's things and the family's history. She was glad for the younger girl when Daniel was satisfied Eli could support a wife and that the house Eli picked out in town was suitable for his sister. The young couple became engaged but were waiting to set a date later in the fall for the wedding.

Jessie was back to work fulltime and wasn't at loggerheads with Daniel as often, beginning to accept Daniel's advice or suggestions as he had his father's. Henry needed to make a decision, and Daniel was giving her space to do so. He hadn't come near her in any intimate way since the evening on the east porch. In fact, Henry hadn't been to that porch since then either.

Jenna came up to Henry one afternoon. "I'd like you to be my maid-of-honor, Henry. I couldn't think of anyone I would want by my side more."

"Oh, Jenna, I'm honored, but you must have girlfriends your own age who you want to stand up with you. Someone who has known you longer, who you giggled over boys with?" Henry asked hoping there was someone the younger girl had overlooked.

"Not really. There weren't very many children my

age when I was in school. A lot of younger girls, but we didn't socialize much although most of them have a crush on Jessie," Jenna confided.

"I have to go home and check on my farm, and the other farmers there depend on me to keep their herds healthy." Henry explained her need to leave to the younger girl. "But I promise to try to come back when you get married in two months." Then she mentally counted on her fingers making sure she would still be able to travel at that time and not be too far along to show although her skirts already felt tight.

"Well, then if you're coming you can be my witness. After all, Daniel has promised to walk me down the aisle so you may as well be part of the wedding," Jenna said reasonably.

"Yes, of course. I'm sure he wouldn't miss it for anything, but I'll have to see how selling the farm goes. Jason, the boy who takes care of things for me, has to go back to school soon. I won't have a lot of time to stay."

There was a commotion out in the yard, and a heavyset older man, wheezing in his anxiety as he pulled his horse to a stop, said breathing hard, "I need the doctor that's here. Boss got gored by a bull, and he's in bad shape. The doc in town is on the other side of the county and ain't expected back for a day or two."

"I'm the doctor, where are you from?" Henry called from the porch.

Shorty came running up from the back yard. "I know, the Circle R. So, was it Herb that got gored?"

"Yep, and he's bleedin' bad. He's as old as I am, and he's in a lot of pain. Looks like a broke arm, too," the older man was able to say now that he caught his

---

breath.

Henry took the lead calling out orders, "Shorty, if you would get a horse for me, I'll get some things I think I'll need." Turning, she entered the house saying, "Jenna, you're in charge of the supper again. It will take me several hours I'd say before I'll be back."

It was only a few minutes and the saddled horse was waiting. Henry found the man calmer after talking with Shorty and knew she had been the topic of their conversation. She learned it was the boss's wife who sent him here to get the doctor, but she hadn't told him it would be a woman.

The two rode off, Henry showing she could keep her seat at the fast pace the older man set for them. Half an hour and they were turning into the wide gate with a Circle R over the entrance. There was a large farm house as well as several outbuildings.

Henry was taken right up to the front steps. Dismounting, she followed the man into the house where she found a gray-haired man, clean shaven except for a trimmed mustache with blood-soaked cloths on his thigh and arm. He was pale, and his face grimaced in pain. A woman of about the same age was hovering over him but had run out of any more ways to keep him comfortable.

"Oh, Henry, I'm so glad you were at home. I'm Nancy Summers, and this is my husband, Herb. We met at the funeral. Ethyl told me how you saved that baby of Emily's, so I knew you could help Herb, too," she said as welcome and stood back so Henry could get to the patient.

Putting on a clean apron, Henry asked to wash her hands. "Also, do you have any alcohol? You know whiskey or brandy? Something strong and pour some in a small bowl for me." Henry lifted the saturated cloths from the leg of the man lying on the leather couch. "Well, I've seen worse. The bull missed your artery, thank God, but I need to get the bleeding stopped before we can work on that arm."

"Dem bull, I should have been payin' more attention to where his interest was. I got between him and his heifers, and I guess he was jealous 'cause I'm better lookin'." Then he grimaced with pain although Henry hadn't touched him, yet.

Henry cut off the trousers from around the wound. "Nancy, would you mind handing me that clean towel and I'll cover his, um, him while I get the thread ready."

Nancy nodded and tucked a towel around her husband's privates then stood back waiting for any other orders Henry may have for her.

"Best give Herb some of the whiskey, too. This is going to take a little while, and it might be best that he isn't sober enough to remember it," Henry suggested, and Herb tipped the bottle to his mouth eagerly with his good arm.

"You're putting the thread and needle in the liquor? I guess that makes sense," Nancy said as she watched Henry begin dabbing at each bleeding spot with some of the alcoholic beverage before finishing with more poured on the gash caused by the horn.

After several minutes, Herb was feeling much better saying, "Now you be careful there, Missy. My man parts are still important to me even if I'm considered over the hill. This dog can still hunt." And he winked at his wife.

Nancy said, "You old coot, if you can joke at a time like this, you're not in too much pain."

"Well, Nance, you can kiss it and make it all better if you want to," he told his wife suggestively.

"Why Herbert Summers, you mind your manners. There's a lady present," she scolded her inebriated husband of at least forty-five years.

"That's no lady. You said she was a doctor. I'm sure she's heard worse." Herb excused his previous conversation.

Henry added to Nancy, "Don't worry, he won't remember what he's said, and I won't repeat it. I would much rather have a happy drunk than one that's ready for a fight, any day. And I'm just about done here with the sutures. I'm going to put on this salve made of honey and turmeric to keep the chance of infection down. I'll show you how to wrap the wound and you need to do the same at least once a day if the pad remains free of blood or a stain."

Nancy nodded as she watched and cut the sleeve of her husband's shirt as Henry instructed. Henry examined the swollen limb from the elbow to the wrist with bruising beginning to show about halfway down. "Give him a little more whiskey, this is going to hurt like hell," Henry said with no apology for her language.

"It's not his first broke bone, but I never seen anything this bad before," Nancy told Henry.

"Hold him down. Don't let his body lift off the couch, sit on him if you need to." Henry grimaced as she took Herb's wrist and hand and placed her foot against the couch and pulled until she felt the bone realign with itself. Herb grunted but didn't yell out although he was sweating profusely by the time Henry was finally pleased with their efforts.

"There, now I'll wrap this arm and I'll mix up some plaster to make sure he can't move or shift it for the next few weeks."

When Henry was happy with the cast and Nancy happy that the medical care was as good as she would have gotten from the regular doctor, Nancy kissed the top of her husband's head and the two women smiled as soft snores emitted from his open mouth.

"I'll come back tomorrow to check on him, but then I'll let the town's doctor take over. I don't want the man to think I'm trying to cut in on his patients. I'm glad I was here to help, but I'm not putting out my shingle," Henry explained with a smile as she went into the kitchen to wash up.

Daniel was sitting at the kitchen table, a half-finished cup of coffee in front of him. He appeared to be relaxed, but Henry got the impression he wasn't at ease.

"Oh, Daniel, I didn't know you were here. I was just about to head back to the ranch," she told him as she cleaned the plaster from her hands.

"No problem. Shorty filled me in when I got back so I hitched up the buggy and came to get you when you were done. Did I understand you don't need to stay the night?" he asked casually.

Henry looked at her husband and knew he was holding something back but continued their conversation in front of Nancy as a loving husband come to pick up his newly wedded wife.

"No, Nancy is going to watch over him." Then she turned to the older woman and finished, "If he gets a fever or the gored area gets hot or red, send for me.

Otherwise, I'll be back tomorrow to change the bandages until Doctor Smith gets back."

"I can't thank you enough, Henry. He would be in such pain if you hadn't been here," Nancy said seriously.

"That's what neighbors are for. Ready to go, Daniel?" Henry said taking the bull by the horn.

"Yep, right behind you," he answered and thanked Nancy for the coffee.

On the ride home, Daniel said, "I'm sorry you got called out on this. I could tell by the pile of bloody rags on the back porch it wasn't a pretty sight in there. But Herb's going to be all right? Maybe have a limp, but all right?" he asked, driving the buggy with her saddled horse tied to the back.

"I could have ridden home. They would have sent someone with me if I didn't think I knew the way," she told him shortly. "I'm capable of getting myself from one place to another alone."

Henry could tell Daniel was trying to weigh his words finally saying, "A lot of things can happen on a little used road like this one. Your horse could bolt, scared by a snake or rabbit, you could get thrown. I don't know, Henry. I don't feel comfortable with you out of the ranch yard without me. Don't try to make this into something like I don't trust you or think you're not capable. I just need to know you're safe, that the baby is safe. I can't explain it more than that," he ended grumpily.

Henry, trying not to start a fight, said conciliatorily, "I understand, although I find it rather suffocating in moments like this. I've always been independent, even when my father was alive. He went his way, and I went mine. We had different interests and rarely saw one another after my mother passed."

"Having someone to watch over, worry about is a little different for me, too. I'm used to not thinking about anyone except myself, but now you and the baby consume my thoughts. I don't mind, in fact I kind of like it, but it's going to take a little time to work out how I'm supposed to find a balance. Can you give me that time, Henry? I don't mean anything by it. I just think it's my job, my duty to protect my family," he told her more reasonably now dusk had fallen and it was like being on the east porch.

Henry did understand and was worried this would get worse not better as she increased, the baby showing more and more, his protectiveness growing. She didn't say anything more, and when they got home, he dropped her off at the front steps.

"Go on in and get settled. Jenna put food up for you. I'd like you to eat something."

Henry shook her head silently as she entered the house and climbed the stairs, ignoring Daniel's suggestion she eat. Instead, she got into her muslin gown and slumped into bed, falling asleep by the time Daniel entered the room sometime after she did.

CHAPTER THIRTEEN

Hearing a horse come into the front yard, Henry glanced out to see the familiar shape of the Major riding in on his big black Morgan. Wondering what he wanted, if she was needed to autopsy some poor, hapless victim again, she hurried down the stairs.

"Major," she said breathlessly as she came out on the porch. "How can I help you?"

"Well, Henry, looking as beautiful as ever. Actually, it was your husband I came to talk with. Nothing for you to worry about," the older man said, dismissing her as merely a Ranger's wife. Something that wouldn't have happened two-months ago, when she was thought of as a coroner, a woman respected in her field.

"Major, what brings you way out here?" called out Daniel as he crossed the yard between the stable and the house, wiping his hands on a bandana as he walked.

"Looking for you, Tanner. I thought you'd get tired of being a farmer and come back to us," the Major said with a smile on his face, but not in his voice.

Tanner shook his head saying, "Long trip for nothing. I made it plain the death of my parents meant a lot of changes for me. I'm needed here. I'm a family man now."

"I know, but we have the Wilcox Gang hold-up

near Laredo, and if they get to Abilene, we'll lose them for sure. I thought you would be interested in helping us get this bunch of criminals," the Major continued.

Daniel turned toward Henry, and she knew he wanted to go with the Major but was afraid of what his leaving would mean for them. It actually wasn't going to change anything so she answered for him, "If you care to wait a few minutes, Daniel can leave with you. Just needs to pack up a few things."

Daniel began to say something in opposition, but then nodded his head and agreed. "I can be ready in a few minutes. Would you like to get a cup of coffee or something? Jenna and Henry usually have pie or cake sitting on the back of the stove."

"Coffee sounds good. I'll have it while you pack up if it's not too much trouble," the older man said as he dismounted and went up the steps to the porch.

Daniel yelled out to the stable for Shorty to get his horse ready for a long trip then went upstairs to pack his saddlebag. Henry stayed busy downstairs with their guest, so Daniel couldn't explain why this particular gang was so important, but he could do that once he had them behind bars. Right now, he had to keep his mind on the job at hand. Extra ammunition and his medical kit had to be added as well as some of Henry's salve.

When Daniel returned to the kitchen, he found Henry and Jenna had packed some provisions for the men to take with them. It would save them from having to make a fire or a formal campsite for the next night or two.

Daniel took Henry into the parlor saying quietly, "If you don't want me to go, I'll stay with you. My main focus is for us to be a family. I can pass on going with the Major."

"I know this is something you want to do and there isn't anything you can't be spared from doing here. Be careful and remember you have a family who will miss you terribly if anything bad occurs," she said and rested her head against him feeling warm against his chest.

"I shouldn't be long, and I'll send a wire from every town I can," he told her knowing how precious every minute with her was.

Jenna hugged him, too, and Jessie came out of the stable walking Daniel's horse then handed the reins to his older brother. "Be careful out there," was all he said, but he appeared to be unhappy at his brother's leaving even though it was supposedly what he wanted. But then maybe that was a lifetime ago. The three Tanners waved the two Rangers off then, like deflated balloons, went back to their usual chores. Each with their mind on other things. Henry went to her room and packed what she felt she would need to take with her. The rest she would have sent to her farm in a few weeks. Saying a silent goodbye to her husband, she knew this would be the easiest way for them to part.

CHAPTER FOURTEEN

Henry was back at her farm for a few days when Jason came running to her, out of breath, but able to tell her his brother, the farrier, had been kicked by one of the stagecoach horses. Henry turned toward the house to grab her medical bag and clean towels from the kitchen. Lifting her skirts, she ran down the main street toward the livery where she knew Jason's brother, Adam, worked.

Two men were already there with Jason, who was bent over his brother now lying on the small cot in a room off the barn-like structure. There was blood covering the young man's face and the front of his shirt hanging open on his chest. Henry kneeled next to him to assess the damage, checking his eyes for the worrying dilated pupils.

Cutting off the shirt, she found a horrific wound, the man's breast all but torn from his body, the underlying muscle and tendons showing plainly. The decision was whether to try to save the breast or remove it now so that it didn't turn gangrenous later.

"I'm going to need more light in here, Jason. Get some lamps if there isn't a window or door to open. Then I'll need you to make sure Adam doesn't move. This is going to take a long time to repair."

Jason jumped to do her bidding. The other men

stood aside and mumbled they would be right outside if she needed them. They seemed uncomfortable around so much blood and the injured man they had always known as being a hard worker. With this kind of wound, it looked as if he would never be able to do those things again.

Jason returned, and Henry asked for more clean water than she found in the pitcher on the washstand. This time she had procured the antiseptic carbolic acid Lister developed so she would have it on hand when such an emergency came up. She cleansed the torn chest, trying to see if she could mend the damage a horse's hoof could do to a human body.

"Let's start here," she told Jason, although the young boy was merely there as moral support. "I have done similar reconstructive surgery so this looks worse than it could have been. The tendons are intact, and I'll sew the tissue back with a few little stitches of cat gut. There," she continued talking as if she were doing a training session back at the teaching hospital she first worked at in Ohio after graduating from the University of Michigan.

"Now it's simply going to take dozens more little stitches to keep the skin closed together to heal with a minor scar. He's lucky he's so young, his type of skin is more likely to heal smoother."

Jason watched with wide eyes. He often accompanied Henry on her visits to heal animals, even ones bleeding from getting caught in wire fencing or attacked by a coyote. Henry knew seeing a human and his own brother, at that, was completely different. Jason was shaking but held Adam just in case he woke up and tried to move due to the pain.

"You mean he'll be all right after this, Doc. You wouldn't go to so much trouble if you didn't think he was going to make it, right?" he asked. She knew the young boy was trying to grasp at anything that would give him hope that Adam was going to live.

"I'm not sure about the concussion, Jason. I mean those things sometimes take time and there can be long lasting problems, but he won't die from this chest wound. It's already stopped bleeding, and I think it will heal underneath with time," she told him. "But he'll need a lot of help to do physical work for several weeks, probably months. I expect you to do everything you can for him."

Jason nodded. "I can do almost everything but putting on the shoes part." Seemingly grasping at the fact Adam would be able to go back to doing the job he loved eventually.

Henry took a minute to glance at Jason's pale face wishing she had a bottle to offer him instead of the clear glass bottle of pure alcohol she used to sterilize the needle and threads.

Spreading her salve over a clean cloth, she laid that across the breast and had Jason help her wrap his brother in strips of muslin to keep the bandage in place. "Now let's see to that head wound. It appears he hit something when the horse kicked him. I don't think the horse's hoof itself came anywhere near his head."

After cleaning the injury, she placed a few stitches to close the wound that had stopped bleeding on its own. Wiping more of the salve on the wound, she covered it lightly with a wrapping around his head. Jason and Henry laid Adam down, covering his body after Jason removed his brother's trousers and boots while Henry took care of the bloody rags and water.

Adam's mother, an older woman, her gray hair pulled tightly back from her face, came into the makeshift room and fell sobbing onto the floor next to Adam's bed, afraid to touch anywhere on his evidently severely damaged body.

"Oh, Adam, don't die, don't die on me, son."

"Please, Mrs. Johnson, don't think he's going to die. Adam was hurt severely, but I think with a little time to heal and rest he'll pull through. I was here quickly, and everything seems good so far. Don't make yourself sick with worry. I'll stay with him until I think he's safely out of the woods then you and Jason can take over," Henry explained reasonably.

"I want the doctor, the real doctor to see to him," the overwrought mother said. "I appreciate you tending to my son when the doctor wasn't here, but he'll come back to town soon and he'll take over. It's not right an unmarried woman touch a young man the way you did. I'll wait here for the doctor."

"That's fine, but I'll need to stay, too, until I know how this concussion is. And I need to explain I am a licensed physician and am a married woman, so no improprieties were crossed. The doctor has known, but since I wasn't practicing on humans, we didn't make it known publicly," Henry told the older woman then left the room to get a breath of cooler evening air and calm herself.

These unfair biases were something she didn't need to deal with as a veterinarian, not once the local farmers found she could save their animals at a reasonable fee. Of course, her track record of saving the goat and dog had made the path smoother, and she was good at medical care, both of animal and human. Now she would decide to either leave the area and become a practicing physician or remain and continue caring for animals.

Jason brought Henry lemonade from her own kitchen then apologized for his mother. "She's kind of old fashion in some ways. My sisters keep telling her she needs to grow with the times, but I don't see it happening. My dad thinks any way she tells him to think. He gets walked all over by her," he said showing his resentment of the position his father took when challenged by his wife.

"Don't look at it like that, Jason. Each couple has their own way. It isn't easy living together and making changes for one another."

"Is that why you came back and Ranger Tanner didn't?" he asked her, appearing serious.

"It's complicated, but I think I told you that before, which is not any kind of real answer. I guess the truth is Tanner and I are two different people with different ways of seeing things. And neither one of us want to change. So, we've decided to agree to disagree as they sometimes say." She finished her drink and set the glass down near the handpump.

Entering the room, the light from the lamps leapt out at Henry and she turned out several leaving the one closest to the cot on. Adam became restless, which Henry took as a good sign since that meant he was feeling pain and discomfort, also meaning he was becoming conscious.

Adam's mother glanced up from where she was kneeling on the rough floorboards and said, "I'm sorry I came in here throwing accusations around. I was actually angry the doctor never seems to be around when he's needed. If you hadn't been here, I can't imagine the pain my Adam would be in, let alone if he would still be alive. I owe you more than an apology, and I'm sorry there's a need at all."

"Don't think anything of it, Mrs. Johnson. When a child is injured a parent feels so helpless, no matter what the age of that child. All we can do is pray and make their hurt, our hurt and try to comfort them as much as we can," Henry told the distraught mother. "Now you have other children you need to care for, so I'll stay here for the night. Jason can sleep nearby and call you if there's a need. If the doctor comes, I'll turn Adam's care over to him."

"There's no need to stop caring for my boy. I was just venting and saying things better left unsaid. I'll be back in the morning with some breakfast, unless you come get me afore then," said the woman, who appeared older than she had just a few hours prior.

Henry spent the night sitting next to the cot knowing if Adam made a movement or noise she would awaken immediately. In the early hours of the next day, Henry noticed a change in Adam's breathing. It became deeper, more relaxed, and Henry knew he would be awake in the morning when his mother came by. She let herself relax, too, but didn't move from her uncomfortable place next to his cot. Tomorrow would be soon enough to get the kinks out of her body, time enough to rest in her own bed while others watched over the patient.

As she predicted, Adam was awake and in pain, but not too much if he didn't try to shift the arm Henry strapped close over his chest to prevent any movement for a while. He had a headache which she gave him willow bark water to ease and allowed his mother to feed him a hearty breakfast. Henry told her not to give him coffee for a few days and to make sure he got plenty of eggs and meat to help with the healing. Mrs. Johnson nodded as Henry told her she was going to be at the farm if she needed anything.

Henry didn't rest much during the day, taking the long walk down to the livery every few hours to make sure Adam didn't have a relapse or the pain hadn't worsened. Everything seemed to be progressing as it should. The 'real' doctor showed up and was there on one of Henry's visits.

In front of Adam's family, the doctor complimented Henry's skill and technique, admiring the small, neat sutures and claiming his wouldn't have been nearly as good. He repeated most of Henry's orders on the care of the patient then went down the street to his own home for some much-needed rest. Henry said she would come by for a visit, but explained now that the doctor was back, Adam was his patient until he recovered full health again.

That night was the first time Henry felt she could relax enough to get some real sleep, knowing she wouldn't be needed by anyone since the doctor was back in town.

CHAPTER FIFTEEN

She awoke to someone in the house, she knew she heard a noise and thinking Adam had need of her called out, "Jason, is that you?"

"No, honey, it's me," said a familiar male voice that made her heart jump merely hearing it.

"Ta, Daniel, I wasn't expecting you. Did you get your man?" she asked remembering why she was there alone in the first place.

There was a hesitation and a sigh then, "Yeah, but can we discuss this in the morning? I'm kinda bushed. I've been walking my horse for the last few miles since it's so dark tonight I couldn't see the road. I was going to sleep in the second bedroom like before, if that's all right."

"Sure, sure that'll be fine. Jason's in the barn, I think," she told him to let him know the second bedroom was vacant.

"I ran into him already, woke him, too, when I put my horse away. I'll see you in the morning."

Henry didn't remember much after that. She didn't even think she dreamt. She knew she felt safe and relaxed and secure and woke more refreshed than she had in weeks, ever since leaving the ranch. She became aware of sounds of someone in her kitchen and the smell of flapjacks in the air.

"I thought the smell of food would have you coming out here eventually. I've already eaten, couldn't wait for a sleepyhead," Tanner said watching as Henry pinked at being made the center of the conversation.

"I had a patient, and I haven't been sleeping as soundly," she explained sniffing the air, probably smelling the maple syrup he had earlier. She sat down as he set a plate of the warm fluffy pile of flapjacks in front of her.

"Jason told me when he came in and I fed him. A little grisly, wasn't it? Jason said he had never seen so much blood and that you took it in stride and ordered everyone about. He said his brother was sewn up and resting in a relatively short amount of time."

He watched as she devoured the food, the first time she had really eaten since he found out about the baby. Evidently, she was feeling better, at least in the mornings, and could keep her food down.

On an aside he continued, "You know the doctor back at the ranch said he could use someone like you to help him in our part of the county, at least. He said there have been so many new ranches that he's run ragged. Ex-military men having been paid with land for fighting in the war are still moving into the area with their families."

"The same could be said for here, but this doctor is much younger than yours. Plus, he has a wife who nurses any patients after a surgery or injury in their home."

"So, you're redundant here as a physician?" Daniel asked slowly, not wanting or prepared to have this conversation yet. He needed his wife to listen and understand why he left her at the ranch. "I want to explain why I went with the Major."

Henry shook her head as she finished the flapjacks saying casually, "You don't owe me an explanation. You're a Ranger and can go whenever you want or need to."

"But I didn't want to, I mean, not exactly." He hesitated, trying to explain what may have looked like abandonment. "The Wilcox gang was responsible for the train derailment that killed my parents."

At learning that, Henry's head came up in surprise before she realized how pulled he must have felt when the Major came for him.

"I, I didn't know there was anything like that tied to their deaths. I thought it was an accident, a loose spike or warped rail, something…" she said quietly and waited as he found the words to tell her the rest.

"That's what was made public. Even the papers were kept in the dark about the actual sabotage. After all, my parents weren't the only ones to die in that crash. The Rangers were called in, and the Major took lead because the gang fled back into Texas and, we thought, on their way to Mexico. They must still have needed money, so they circled back up to Laredo gathering more men. To pay that many men, there had to be a big payload they had their eye on, and that limits the number of targets."

"You said last night you got your man. Did you catch the band of men that did this?" she asked holding her breath, praying that Daniel was now free to stay at the ranch if he wanted.

"Yes, killed most of them in a shoot-out as they tried to rob a train near the border as it passed into California. Gold going to the mint. There were about ten of us and fifteen of them, but they were completely blind-sided. We were following one of the newer members, and he was dumb enough to brag to one of the saloon girls who came to us and sold her information," Tanner explained as he seemed to relive the events.

"We were spread out, but lucky enough to get several of the gang members together. They started shooting rather than surrender. Of course, they were facing hanging, so there wasn't much of a reason not to try to shoot their way out.

"The Major had pretty much the same thing happen with his group of men. We ended up with a couple of prisoners, but they were new to the gang and not part of the train derailment at all. They'll go to prison for a few years and get out and try it all over again."

Henry thought about what Daniel told her and realized how difficult it was for him to keep this information from her and his siblings. "Have you told Jessie and Jenna yet? Did they know?"

"I didn't want them to worry or fret if we didn't catch these men. They need to get on with their lives, and the easiest way for them was if they thought of it as an accident, because that's what it was. The Wilcox crew never meant for that much carnage or the cars to overturn. In fact, there was so much damage at the site of the crash, they couldn't even get the gold they were after," he explained, but she didn't find the irony.

"Are you going to tell them now?"

"Probably not, or at least not for years. It wouldn't change their loss." His eyes hungered for her. "I just felt I needed to tell you. I wanted you to know why I left with the Major. That it was for the last time. I've resigned from the Rangers and have no need to find revenge any longer. The bushwhackers who caused the crash that killed my parents are dead. Now my life is all about you and our child."

He hesitated, saying, "I would like to go back to the ranch for Jenna's wedding, but I'll come right back home to you, I promise."

"I promised to attend, too, and she needs family around her at a time like that. It won't be a hardship, but I'm hoping I'm not showing too much. It will make things so much more complicated if people notice my condition," she said placing her hand over her still flat belly.

Daniel's eyes followed her hand liking what he saw, what he thought about when he looked at her there in front of him. "Do you think we could try again? I promise not to pressure you into anything you don't want or aren't ready for."

He pulled her toward him, and she let him. He nuzzled into her hair saying, "I've missed you...this...so much it practically un-mans me, overwhelms me with the extent of my feelings for you."

He kissed her when she gazed up at him, her eyes begging him to. She tasted sweet, like the maple syrup she'd just eaten, but it was ambrosia to Daniel. He paused, wanting to hold Henry while at the same time giving her the option of walking away from him if she wanted.

The two were just getting reacquainted when a voice interrupted them. "Doc? Ma sent over a fresh baked apple pie," Jason said from the doorway.

Daniel broke reluctantly away from Henry as she answered, "Thank you, Jason, please bring it in here.

But tell her she doesn't need to keep baking me things. They all taste so good I'll be big as a house in no time."

Daniel tried to hide the smile that came across his face as she told Jason that and Jason politely declined to comment on it.

"She's so sure you saved Adam and is sorry for ever doubting you." The young boy explained the bounty of baked goods lining the counter.

"Now that Daniel's here, they may disappear faster than before." Then she changed topics. "Is Adam's headache finally getting better?"

"Yep, he's sitting up and walking to the privy, stuff like that so I think he'll be back to ordering me around any day now." Jason smiled as he backed out the door. "Glad to see you back, Ranger Tanner." Then he disappeared out the door with a big grin on his face.

"I think he saw us," Henry said with a smile. "But he'll never tell anyone else."

"No, but he's told me a thing or two." At Henry's questioning look he went on to explain. "I've been chewed out for leaving you unmarried and with child, for not following you quickly enough both times you left me, for forcing you to be unhappy, and for not making it clear to everyone in town that we are married and everything done in this house is aboveboard."

Then he laughed outright at Henry's expression of mortification that a fourteen-year-old boy took him to task over their relationship.

"He hasn't said quite as much to me, but he knew I was expecting almost before I did." At Daniel's questioning expression, she explained, "Jason has seven younger siblings and was very observant of his mother's condition each time." They both smiled over her young protector.

"Well, he has a point, Henry. If you stay here, we're going to have to let people know I'm not just shacking up with you. And once you start to..." He pointed at her stomach. "You know, get bigger, I don't want any talk about you and our child."

"I've still been thinking of selling, even though there is less reason to now. Adam is planning on getting married, and Jason talked about me selling the farm to Adam on time with half down. He wants to keep being the farrier in town, and this is so close, he can have a home farm without needing to ride in to the livery every day. It sounds perfect for him and Annie, then I could move to someplace in need of a doctor."

She seemed to plead at him. "Can we speak of something else for a while, Daniel? I haven't made up my mind, and I don't want to do so when I'm emotional."

"So, you're emotional, are you? Do I have anything to do with that?" He pulled her back to him, pressing his hips into hers, watching her eyes as they darkened with desire, which almost made him pick her up and carry her to the bedroom. But he didn't. He reminded himself he would go slowly with her. It had to be her decision. Anything else would spell disaster for their marriage. He paused, wanting to hold Henry, but at the same time giving her the option of coming to him if she wanted.

"I need to think about this rationally and yes, you disturb me in ways I don't always feel comfortable with," she told him honestly.

Daniel spread his arms into the air. His hands wide open in surrender. "I'm not doing anything if you don't want me to. I just want to be near you to make sure you're safe, that's all." Then to give her some breathing space, he asked, "Is there anything that needs to be done, maybe getting ready for the fall harvest?"

She seemed to think. "We noticed a porcupine has been chewing a large hole in the bottom of the corn shed, and Jason doesn't know how to go about fixing it. And there are shingles blown off the shed's roof. Jason might have other ideas. He tries to keep things up, but he's only fourteen, even if he does seem so much older at times," she explained. "I usually pay his brother to do some of the more difficult jobs, but Adam won't be up to doing any for a while."

He gave her a brief kiss. "I'll see you at supper, and don't eat all that pie. It smells delicious from here." He grabbed his hat off the hook by the door as he left.

After supper and two pieces of pie each, Henry disappeared into her bedroom. Daniel knew the time to discuss all the difficult things had finally arrived. He didn't want to leave for Jenna's wedding without knowing if he was to be a married man or not. He prayed Henry would give him this chance, the chance to prove himself. Prove he could be a husband and father. Anything to convince her they should remain a family.

Standing in front of the almost closed door, he tapped on it as it swung open for him to see her standing there, indecision plainly on her face. He came in, glancing around at the neat room with its pretty bed cover and corner chair covered in flowered chintz.

Grinning, he asked, "Remember the porch rocking chair?" He knew she did when her cheeks went rosy. "It doesn't have to be that particular chair. We can start our own traditions, and I like this chair just fine."

Henry allowed him to pull her across his lap as he sat down. Her head close to his chest as she relaxed into his body liking the way she fit perfectly. She could hear his heartbeat and the rumble of his voice as he spoke.

"I don't plan on leaving you and the baby," he stated. "When you made your move on me back in Melville, I thought I was the luckiest S.O.B. on the planet. I couldn't believe you had that kind of interest in me, but I wasn't going to turn you down. That was my chance to show you how much I cared."

"I didn't make my move on you," she disavowed. "That suggests I planned on doing what we did, and I didn't, not really. But I did want to be close to you, know what it's like to be made love to, feel you in me," she confided quietly.

Daniel moved uncomfortably under her. "Honey, if we're to have this conversation, please keep to the facts or my self-control will crumble."

"I am sticking to the facts, but I understand what you mean. Not so graphic."

"Exactly," he nodded. "My feelings for you haven't changed. They began as something I thought was going to pass, especially after you were gone, but that wasn't how it happened. I wanted to have you near me. So much so I sent away for my grandmother's rings hoping you missed me enough to marry me. Then I find you pregnant with my child, and that sealed the deal. I can't leave you, Henry. I love you, and I love this baby."

He placed his hand on her stomach leaving it there protectively. "I don't know what I can do to prove it to you, or is it that you don't think you can ever love me?"

His voice held a hint of hurt.

Unsure how to treat Daniel, as a husband or a friend, she hesitated. He was both and she loved that about him, but could she be a wife?

"I'm not sure I know what love is, Daniel, not that kind of love, I mean. I missed you, but I'm also afraid of giving up my independence. I get lost in you," she confessed her fears.

"But that's what couples do—get lost in each other. We become one in more ways than just our bodies." He stroked her back. "That's one of the things I like about being with you. I like how you think, that you can argue with me and not hold it against me if I don't agree. I like how you melded right in with Jenna and Jessie, like you'd known them for years."

He shifted her toward his chest so her face was inches from his. "I don't see why any of that scares you. What have I done that makes you think I'll push you to do anything you don't want?" Then added, "Besides staying married that is."

"Perhaps I'm looking at this all wrong. I like you touching me, I like talking with you, especially, in this chair. And I know I can trust you to take care of me and our child, but then what am I? A wife? A mother-to-be?" she asked confused.

"You're what you've always been. A beautiful, desirable woman who is highly skilled as a physician and veterinarian, independent enough to run a farm and work as a medical examiner for the Texas Rangers. You're the woman I love, the mother-to-be of our child, and I hope my lover. I know you'll be great at all of the last three if you give us a chance." She didn't doubt his sincerity when she gazed into his eyes.

"I think you just happened to me at a time I was beginning to question my original plan of turning away from doctoring people. I think I need to get back to doing that, not wasting the education and talent I have. I need to be brave enough to face the fact I won't be able to save everyone, but I can give them a better chance and the best care possible."

She knew deep down she was right. It hadn't been Daniel but facing those dead women knowing she could have made their life better, safer if she had known them sooner.

"So, are you saying you and I are all right? You don't have a problem with me staying here with you?" Daniel asked tentatively.

Henry was quiet for a few minutes, rolling everything they said around in her mind. She came to the realization she wasn't afraid of what Daniel would ask of her at all or that he would fail her in some way. She was afraid she would come to love them all and, like her mother then her father, they would leave her to live alone with her pain.

"I agree with your original argument. We belong together, and everything else will fall into place. I love you, Daniel Warren Tanner. But I have plans. I think we should live at the ranch for at least the next few years until Jessie knows what he wants to do. I think I'm a good doctor, better than most, so I will return to my profession until I have so many children, I can't handle both," she told him, gazing up into his happy blue eyes. "I'm sorry it took me so long to realize what I had in you. Thank you for giving me so many chances to find my love for you."

"I wasn't going anywhere, Darlin', but this sure

takes a weight off my shoulders knowing we're going to be a family. Now let's see if we remember how to make love." He lifted her easily and carried her toward the bed.

A word about the author...

Susan Payne has been reading since a young age. She credits her husband for the inspiration of the men in her stories. Usually, a man of action rather than words. The rest is pure fiction and a lot of psychology. Contact her through:

http://www.authorsusanpayne.com